The Anchor of the Soul

Soul

Tales of African American

Rhode Island

JAMES DOHERTY

For Gary Adams

Contents

Preface

I was utterly captivated by a remarkable portrait in the collection of the Rhode Island Historical Society. The portraitist, John Blanchard, admirably captured the confidence and air of authority of his sitter, Thomas Howland. A handsome man with dashingly upswept hair, Howland gazes quizzically at the viewer, a distinct glint of challenge in his eye. Not the least thing that is remarkable about this painting from the 1850s is that Thomas Howland looks supremely comfortable in his own Black skin.

The portrait prompted many questions. Who was this man? What was his occupation? How was it that he exuded such confidence? How, in the 1850s, did his portrait come to be painted at all? The quest for answers to these questions led to the discovery of a rich and unexpected history.

The fictional stories in this collection chronicle the lives of real people. Thomas Howland was a renowned businessman in Providence, whose election to municipal office in 1857-- the result of a joke-- attracted national attention. The events of his life, and of its most momentous year, happened substantially as I recount them. An intimate glimpse into Newport Gardner's life is offered here. Born Okyerema Mireku in Africa around 1746, "Newport" was enslaved for thirty years but nonetheless became a civic leader and noted composer of music, some of which can be listened to online today. My tale of the voyage of the Newport slaving vessel, *Little George*, follows the vivid account of her captain, and though my story set in the nineteenth-century African American ghetto of Snow Town is entirely fictional, there really was such a place, much as I describe it, situated on what is now the Rhode Island State House lawn. This is a collection of stories telling of courageous lives lived amid a dark history, tracing a line from slavery and segregation to second-class citizenship in the present day.

Slave owners and traders depicted in these pages, men like Aaron Lopez, Rowland Robinson, George Scott, and Nathaniel Briggs—all God-fearing Christians and Jews-- were historical figures, who, in broad terms, played the roles that I have cast them in. The words that I have put in their mouths, however, are a distillation of words and ideas from the historical record, expressed by a variety of men engaged in the transatlantic slave trade. My aim in these stories is not to pass judgment, but to cast light on the beliefs, attitudes, and motivations that made one of the most violent enterprises in all of history possible, ideas that cast a shadow that reaches us today.

We in the United States often think of slavery as a phenomenon of the American South that somehow did not touch the Northern colonies (and later, states). Northerners often cherish a sense of moral superiority, celebrating a history of tolerance and liberality, untarnished by slavery. Yet this notion is entirely false, in no case more so than Rhode Island's. Rhode Island men were heavily engaged in the African slave trade, an occupation considered perfectly respectable for a large part of the eighteenth century. From trading in slaves in the colonial era to the later manufacture of Kersey or negro cloth, supplied to Southern plantation owners, the fortunes derived directly and indirectly from African slavery helped to establish the elites who dominated the state in the nineteenth and twentieth centuries.

The history of Black people in Rhode Island dates to within a few decades of the colony's foundation in 1636. The twelve commissioners of the General Court of Election for Providence and Warwick resolved in 1652 that "no blacke mankind or white" should be held in perpetual slavery. The resolution, the first of its kind in North America, proved a dead letter from the start. In 1680, Governor Peleg Sanford recorded "blacks" as a distinct group in the colony. By 1755, the Black population of Rhode Island numbered 4,697, or eleven per cent of the population.

In South Kingstown, where enslaved African men and women worked on the sprawling agricultural estates of the Narragansett Planters, they made up nearly a fifth of the population. King's County, as Washington County was then known, was one of a handful of places in the American colonies outside the South where plantation slavery operated on any scale. Though the number of enslaved people employed on these plantations was no more than forty or so per farm, slave labor enabled the two dozen landowning families of King's County to live in the opulent style of the English gentry. The miles of stone walls traversing the woodlands of southern Rhode Island, many built by enslaved Africans, are a testament to the vastness of the pasturelands upon which enslaved people once toiled.

Clustered in settlements around the magnificent harbor of Narragansett Bay, it was natural that the colonists of Rhode Island should look to the sea to make their way in the world. Trade was the colony's lifeblood, and for more than a century and a half of its history, Rhode Island was at the fore of a sophisticated complex of industries-- maritime, agricultural, artisanal, manufacturing, financial-- built upon the trade in enslaved people and sustaining the institution of slavery.

Of all the British North American colonies engaged in the transatlantic slave trade, tiny Rhode Island's share was the largest. Of 1,600 recorded slave journeys originating from the territory of the United States prior to 1808, when the importation of slaves was banned, an astonishing fifty-nine per cent of the voyages embarked from Rhode Island.[1] Nearly 47,000 African men, women, and children were recorded to have been transported to

---

[1] Data extracted from www.slavevoyages.com

the New World on Rhode Island vessels, though as fewer than half of the human cargoes of those slave vessels were enumerated, the true figure is almost certainly more than 100,000. By my estimate, the revenue generated for shipowners from *just one leg* of the triangular trade—the infamous Middle Passage, westward from Africa-- totaled £2,500,000 over the course of a century, no less than three hundred million dollars in today's money, and possibly much more.

Yet slave trading only accounted for perhaps twenty per cent of the colony's maritime activity in the eighteenth century. Far more important was the coastal trade, transporting Rhode Island's produce north and south, which was traded for goods like Virginia tobacco or Newfoundland salted cod, commodities that could be stored for onward shipment and traded elsewhere. The colony's largest town, the port of Newport, became a clearing house second in New England only to Boston for the manifold produce and wares of the British North American colonies.

Rhode Island's most vital trade link was with the islands of the West Indies, where the practice of slavery was at its most brutal. Overseers with machetes were positioned by the sugar cane presses there, ready to hack off the limbs of enslaved people caught in the machinery. The life expectancy of enslaved people who toiled in the cane fields averaged just seven years. Mortality was so high that only the regular importation of slaves from Africa could sustain the islands' populations. So profitable was growing sugar cane in the Caribbean that no land could be spared for grazing or growing foodstuffs. The livestock and produce of the Narragansett Planters, conveyed by Newport's substantial merchant fleet, sustained the West Indies' staggeringly lucrative monoculture.

Famed Narragansett Pacer horses turned the cane mills that extracted juice for molasses. Rhode Island vessels transported tainted salted cod from Newfoundland to the islands of the Caribbean, where it served as the staple protein of the enslaved people on the sugar plantations. Rhode Island cornmeal and beans supplemented their diet, and salt fish, beans, and cornmeal remain much-loved features of West Indian cuisine to this day.

Sea captains returned from the Caribbean islands with Rhode Island's most prized import: dark amber molasses, which the alchemists of Newport's twenty-two distilleries turned into gold. Rhode Island rum, or killdivil, as it was known, was transported in large quantities to the African coast in the eighteenth century. So precious was rum as a medium of exchange for African slaves that the workmen of Newport complained that there was seldom a drop to be had in the town.

Most African captives were transported to the West Indies or sold in Southern ports like Charleston; some, however, returned with the slave vessels to Rhode Island. There emerged two distinct populations of enslaved people in the colony: the agricultural laborers of the Narragansett Planters and other places, and the town slaves of Newport. The character of slavery in Newport was unusual, if not unique in colonial America. Large numbers of enslaved men crewed vessels or labored on the docks or as craftsmen in workshops there, as they did in other ports. In Newport, however, there were also highly skilled enslaved men, whose talents appear to have been cultivated from a young age, working as bookkeepers, secretaries, or artisans. One was even a master chocolate maker. This elite of literate enslaved men could earn money in time "gained" for diligent work, rent homes, and acquire possessions, all while remaining the property of their owners. An emergent Black intelligentsia of free and newly freed men in the town formed the Free African Union Society in 1780, the first African American mutual aid society in North America.

The Revolutionary War severed Rhode Island's trade routes, and its economy collapsed. Newport's Golden Age was never to return. With trade at a standstill, many enslaved people were freed, their services no longer required. Gradual emancipation came in 1784, and many more slaves were released from bondage. People valued for their labor as slaves became valueless as free men and women. Chased out of town after town, Black Rhode Islanders mostly settled in Providence, where they eked out a marginal existence in ghettos like Hardscrabble and Snow Town. Even in these wretched havens they were scorned and harassed by the predominant White population, their settlements being attacked by violent mobs in 1824 and 1831.

Prior to the Civil War, the proportion of Rhode Island's Black population to its White was the highest of any Northern state, but the rising tide of industrialization that lifted many boats in the nineteenth century left African Americans high and dry. The gates of the great factories like Gorham's, Nicholson File, and Brown & Sharpe were firmly closed to Blacks, and domestic service positions formerly open to them were increasingly filled by Irish immigrants. With the exception of Black seamen, who enjoyed an unusual degree of equality with their White shipmates, hardly any Black Rhode Islanders worked in skilled trades, or would have been welcome had they applied. Appalling living conditions, inadequate sanitation, and non-existent medical care meant that, in the mid-nineteenth century, the death rate of Providence's Black population was twice that of the surrounding community. Not for nothing is the period between the 1870s and World War I known as the nadir of the African American experience.

These important, but little-known facts about American history deserve to be widely taught and discussed because they illuminate our present as much as our past. Slavery, which played such an enormous role in Rhode Island's history, is, I believe, not just a deplorable memory, but a living fact in our lives. It lives on in laws and institutions constructed to accommodate African slavery, and in smaller, but highly consequential ways, like pernicious ideas embedded deep in our consciousnesses, ideas that account, in part, for the stark racial wealth gap that persists in the United States today.

It is sometimes said that we share a common history but have different memories. In the centuries-long agony of slavery, and the century and a half of rejection, neglect, and stagnation that followed, countless numbers of those different memories were obliterated, leaving it to the imagination of the writer of fiction to attempt to revive them. I like to think that these pages give voice to some of those different memories, attending to voices all but lost to oblivion, people whose stories remind us that the struggle for freedom and equality remains unfinished business.

Certain anecdotes, witticisms, and background characters in these pages are taken from Thomas Hazard's 1879 *The Jonny-Cake Papers of "Shepherd Tom"*, recounting tales of Washington County life and folklore from the late eighteenth and early nineteenth centuries. These include the character (whom I hope was real) of a Black transgender woman named Nancy Brown, who boldly decided to live life on her own terms in the Washington County of the early 1800s.

For the sake of authenticity in describing the eras in which these stories are set, the terms used to describe African Americans follow the antiquated conventions of their times, which some readers may find offensive.

Black Tom

1857

The clank of the blacksmith's hammer halted when the astonishing news reached the South Water Street wharf. Carters set down their barrows. The grog dens and oyster houses fell silent. The cargoes of cranes were suspended in mid-flight. Then a great gale of laughter swept over the waterfront. Black Tom had been elected to public office!

Everybody in the city of Providence knew Black Tom. Standing six feet four inches tall, with a stalwart physique, Tom Howland was larger than life in every respect. He was said to be the strongest man in Rhode Island, able to carry barrels of flour under his arms as easily as if they were a pair of kittens. Renowned as a believer in law and order, Tom once seized three miscreants, caught red-handed, and so terrified a fourth that the rascal led them all to the College Street lock-up.

Black Tom's extraordinary election was the result of an elaborate joke. At a primary election on April 1, a young Democrat named Davis realized that the Republicans had blundered in electing a warden to supervise the election day poll by a voice vote, when the law required that such officials be elected by ballot. It would be a terrific joke, this Davis thought, to elect the celebrated Black Tom as warden and the wealthy banker Zechariah Tucker in the subordinate role of clerk. Saying nothing to arouse suspicion, Davis wrote out a few ballots and gave them to his friends, who deposited them in the ballot box. When the box was emptied, the counters were mystified to find among the ballots five for Tom Howland for warden and the same number for Tucker as clerk. Great was the wrath and mortification of the Republicans when they learned that these were the only legal votes that had been cast. They had made April Fools of themselves. A colored man had been elected warden!

Tom Howland was shutting up his warehouse for the day when a breathless Charlie Hoxsie came running up with the news.

"You been elected! You been elected warden!" Charlie cried.

"Warden? What are you talking about?" asked Tom.

"It's true. You been elected!"

"Charlie Hoxsie, you done lost your senses. No colored man's ever been elected nothin."

"It's true! I swear! Someone played some kinda joke or somethin, but you're sure as hell a warden, whatever that is."

Tom grabbed his hat and he and Charlie strode into the street. People leaned out of their windows to wave and hoot and whistle as the two men hurried toward Tom's house.

A stevedore since the age of thirteen, Tom Howland had, thanks to his sharp wits, long since ceased hauling cargoes himself but employed other men to do so, building, over thirty years, the first stevedoring firm of any consequence in Providence. Visitors to the city gaped at the sight of a towering black man shouting orders at teams of white men.

Seeing the waste from the levelling of Fox Point Hill in the 1830s, young Tom shrewdly struck upon the idea of using the rubble as ballast for oceangoing sailing vessels. He carted away the soil, hired men to break rocks and screen the shingle, and sold it to mariners and shipowners. This reaped Tom a rich harvest, enabling him to open a tavern on Market Square and construct one of the finest houses in the city for himself on Wickenden Street.

Tom Howland took seriously the responsibility that success and prominence conferred. With caterer George T. Downing and other leading men of the community, Tom organized a Council of the Colored People of Rhode Island, dedicated to maintaining the rights of the black citizens of the state. At a time when slaves still toiled in the American South, Tom Howland's was a forceful voice in the fight to attain greater equality at home.

The rise of steam power heralded a slow decline of Tom's business enterprises. Steamships, with their iron keels, had less need for ballast, and that side of his business slumped. In the wake of side-wheel steamers came steam cranes that sprouted up all along the riverfront, and wharves that once bustled with the shouts and shanties of Tom's men now hissed and clanged with the sounds of pistons and gears. Tom was forced to close the tavern on Market Square. One by one the mortgages on his rental properties were foreclosed. The splendid house on Wickenden Street fell into disrepair.

Now in his fifties, Tom resorted to trading on his celebrity, entering the harness races at Washington Park, clad in garish costumes. Though Tom was popular with racegoers, he was no jockey, and he never won the fifty-dollar purse. Those in the city who resented Tom Howland's outspokenness and pride were not displeased that the celebrated Black Tom's fortunes appeared to be sliding.

Tom's wife Alice and daughter Mary were chatting excitedly with friends outside in the street when Tom and Charlie arrived at the house.

"Is it true, papa?" Mary asked, rushing up to her father.

"I dunno," replied Tom.

"It's true," confirmed Henry Brown, Judge Angell's coachman. "I jus heard it off the judge. He din't look one bit happy."

"You must be the first colored man elected in the history of the whole United States!" Mary exclaimed.

As more well-wishers arrived, drawn by the news, the lawyer, Thomas Millett, rode up, looking pink-faced and flustered. He dismounted clumsily, almost falling in the process.

"Evening, Mr. Millett," Tom greeted him.

"You've heard the news, I see," Millett sniffed. "It's all just a misunderstanding. There's no need to worry, I will have it cleared up by morning."

"Nothing worrying me, sir," Tom replied. "What's in need of clearing up?"

"Well, I mean, obviously it was not the intention…" began Millett. "What I mean to say is… I mean, anyone can see it was just a prank," the lawyer said, fumbling in his coat pocket for some papers. "So, if you will just sign this affidavit," he continued, "renouncing your claim--"

"Mr. Millett," Tom interrupted, "I thank you kindly. And I appreciate what a great joke it was, a prank as you call it, to elect a colored man to office. Well, sir, I thank you for your courtesy in stopping by, but I'll tell you what I'm inclined to do. I'm minded to march down to City Hall tomorrow morning, and if I have to speak to the mayor himself, I am going to demand to be sworn into office."

A whoop went up among the throng, and people danced with joy. Millett rode off, looking miserable.

Spectators flocked to Pioneer Hall on election day, two weeks later, to witness the spectacle of Black Tom supervising the poll. Tom raised his hat cheerily as he arrived, bounding up the steps. The hall bustled with many more people than the propertied men who were entitled to vote. Tom took his place, seated beside the lavishly bewhiskered Zechariah Tucker. The portly, ruffle-shirted financier was sweating profusely, unable to conceal his embarrassment. After a few formalities, Tom declared the poll open.

It was a custom passed down from "old colony days" for men to raise their hats as they came forward to deposit their ballots, and the first few voters did just that. Then came the turn of the crotchety South Water Street merchant, William Earle, well known for his gruff manner.

"Do they all take their hats off to you, Tom?" Earle growled.

"'cording to how they've been brought up, sir," came Tom's reply, quick as a flash.

The hall erupted in laughter. Old Earle, red-faced, grunted and curtly doffed his hat.

Tom comported himself with dignity, and the day passed without further incident. When the poll closed at four o'clock, Tom counted the ballots, cross-checked his tally with Tucker's, and in a clear voice, he declared the Republican, J.N. Francis, the winner. The assembled spectators cheered, as much for Black Tom's good-humored discharge of his duties as for the victorious candidate.

The portrait over the mantelpiece cast its penetrating gaze over Tom Howland's dining room that evening. Tom, a little grayer and heavier than his image in the portrait, recounted the day's events to Alice and Mary at the dinner table.

"At least they were respectful," Alice said.

"It was a great big joke to them," Tom responded. "A colored warden! Ha, ha, ha. People only came expecting me to make a fool of myself."

"Well, you didn't," Mary said.

Tom grabbed a bottle of whiskey and swiftly downed a glass.

"And the joke was made even funnier by the Dred Scott business. I tell you, that decision has really gotten under my skin," he said, reaching for a weeks-old newspaper.

"Not that again," Alice pleaded.

Tom read aloud from the newspaper.

"*The Dred Scott case,*" he boomed. "*Judgment of Chief Justice Taney ... Negroes had no rights which the white man was bound to respect ... A perpetual and impassable barrier was intended to be erected between the white race and the one which they had reduced to slavery.*"

"It can't stand, papa," insisted Mary.

"It's the Supreme Court of the United States!" Tom cried. "Telling a man freeborn on the American soil"— he choked on the words as he uttered them— "telling *me* that I am not a *citizen*?"

Tom poured another glass of whiskey and gulped it down.

"My father fought a war for liberty," he seethed. "Liberty for what? For the liberty of the white man to enslave the black? To deny us our rights as citizens, as people? *That* is what the Supreme Court has said."

"Every effort we make is thwarted," he fumed, "every hand offered in friendship is turned away. We show ourselves to be *ever loyal* and are *ever betrayed*. We are going backward in this country!"

"Tom," Alice said, grasping his hand. "Life will go on. It will be okay."

Tom shook his head vehemently.

"No, honey, it will not be okay," he said. "I don't think things will ever be okay in this country."

"It will pass," Alice insisted. "Trade will pick up soon, and you'll be out of this awful slump you're in."

"Stevedoring business isn't coming back. A steam crane and three men can unload a hold that used to take a gang of fifteen."

"You still might win in the races one day," Mary suggested.

"Is that my future?" Tom asked. "As a sideshow freak? Dressing up as Uncle Sam at the clambakes at Fields Point? I'll be damned if I'll be a white man's figure of fun for the rest of my days. If I ever hear monkey noises again like I hear at that racetrack, I swear I'll knock some damned fool's teeth out."

"Please, please, stop," Alice begged. "This kind of talk gets you nowhere."

Tom mused silently for a moment.

"Maybe Reverend Crummell is right," he said at length.

"What?" Alice exclaimed.

"Maybe he's right," Tom continued. "Maybe we should face facts. This land is not for us. Maybe we should join him in Liberia."

"Thomas Howland, I can't believe my ears. This land is our home!" Alice cried. "You yourself have said so many times, anytime that anyone ever suggested the idea of negroes leaving."

"The colonization people say that we can live freer in Africa than we can ever hope to here," Tom replied. "And for the first time, you know, I think they may be right."

"But you said that those people hate us," Alice countered.

"They want us to leave, a lot of abolitionists do."

"Not all of them do. And anyway, if things are so bad, why don't you talk to one of your rich abolitionist friends?" suggested Alice.

"About what?" asked Tom.

"About some kind of *job*, here in Providence."

"It's not about a job, it's about our future! Mary's future. Let me tell you something about the abolitionist and "great friend of the negro", Mr. Lucien Sharpe. Now Mr. Sharpe has always been highly courteous to me. But there's three hundred men at that factory of his, and how many of em-- besides janitors or watchmen— how many of em do you think are colored? Not one. Not one, Alice."

"But you're not just any colored man, you're Tom Howland!"

"That Supreme Court ruling says *no* colored man's as good as a white man," Tom insisted. "No, I'm seriously minded to write to Reverend Crummell and tell him that we're ready to come to Liberia."

"Tom Howland, you know I will follow you anywhere, to the poorhouse or the gates of Hell. But is it fair to do this to Mary? What about her future, her prospects for marriage?"

"What future does Mary have here?"

"I *want* to go, Momma," Mary said. "I could teach the people there."

"You don't know nothing about Africa, child," Alice snapped.

"We know that I'll be a man there," Tom said. "Not less than a man. Not even a colored man. Just a man. For the first time in my life."

Alice's eyes welled with tears.

"Tom," she said, squeezing his hand, "I'm scared. This whole idea of leaving for Africa scares me."

"I know," Tom confessed. "It scares me, too, a little. But think about it. What's left for us here? What future is there for Mary, or for any colored man or woman with things as they are?"

Fiercely devoted to Tom though she was, Alice was determined to get him to reconsider his decision. The next morning, she resolved what she would do. Putting on her Sunday-best dress, she caught a horsecar across town and walked to the gates of a vast red-brick mill. Towering over the factory roof were letters that spelled out ORRAY TAFT & CO. Alice summoned up her nerve and marched to the gatehouse.

"My name is Mrs. Tom Howland, and I'm here to see Mr. Orray Taft," Alice announced to the stunned watchman. No colored woman aside from a cleaning lady had ever called at the factory gates before, much less asked to see the president of the spinning mill.

The watchman sent a messenger to Mr. Taft's office on the third floor, and to his astonishment received a reply directing him to admit the visitor. Alice was escorted upstairs, past the rows of staring eyes of clerks and bookkeepers and guided to the office of Mr. Orray Taft. Taft greeted Alice warmly.

"I'm delighted to meet you, Mrs. Howland, though I can't imagine why you've come to see me," he said. "What can I do for you?"

"Thank you for seeing me, Mr. Taft. I know you hold Tom in some esteem."

"I certainly do."

"Well, sir, I don't want to take up too much of your time, so I'll come straight to the point," Alice said. "Tom has got it into his head that we should leave for Liberia."

"Emigrate!" exclaimed Taft. "Whatever for? Tom is the best-loved man in the city. A credit to his race in every respect, and an example for colored boys. We can't afford to lose a man like him."

"Thank you, sir, but he doesn't see it that way. Business has been poor in the stevedoring trade with the new machinery and all…"

"I expect so."

"And well, Mr. Taft," Alice continued, "there's another reason as well. Tom was crushed by that Dred Scott decision, just crushed. For a man like Tom to be told he's not a citizen! Well, sir, that's just an insult he can't bear."

"It's dreadful. Every fair-minded man I know is appalled by it. But why should Tom take it personally?"

Alice's eyes flashed with anger.

"How could any colored man with an ounce of pride not take it personal?" she said.

"No, of course," replied Taft. "It was a foolish thing to say. But what can I do? Offer him a job?"

"Well, sir, Tom's so proud and so used to being his own boss, that I was thinking--"

"I've got it," Taft interjected. "Excuse me, Mrs. Howland, but there is something that might persuade him to stay. The post of harbor master for the port of Providence is coming to the end of its term shortly. The present occupant must be at least a hundred years old."

"Harbor master!"

"Yes, I and some prominent men from the waterfront could petition the city council on Tom's behalf and provide him with letters of recommendation. I couldn't guarantee he'd get the job, of course, but it would be sure to sway the council's decision."

Alice's eyes filled with tears.

"You'd do that for Tom?" she asked.

"I'll draft the petition personally."

"Oh, Mr. Taft, I can't thank you enough."

"I'll do it gladly," Taft said. "I can't imagine Providence without Tom Howland. He's been a legend in this city since I was a boy. He must be persuaded to stay."

A large envelope was delivered a few days later. Alice, guessing the contents, put it on the dining room table. She could hardly contain her excitement as Tom opened the packet when he arrived home that evening. His eyes grew wide as he read.

"Harbor master!" he exclaimed. "A petition to the city council?

Mr. Salsbury, Mr. Taft, Mr. Bailey, all writing letters of support? What? How?" Tom asked.

Alice and Mary, who by now was in on the secret, could not stifle giggles.

"What?" Tom demanded. "What is it?"

"I went to see Mr. Taft and told him of your plan to emigrate to Liberia, and he said you had to be persuaded to stay. He thought this was the best way of making you think again," Alice explained.

"Mr. Taft? You went to see Mr. Taft?"

"Mm-hmm."

Tom's expression grew stern.

"You had no business going to see Mr. Taft. I've made a definite decision about leaving. I even applied for passports so that Mary can come back one day if she wants to," he said.

"Mr. Taft said you were the best-liked man in the entire city and ought to stay."

"He did?" Tom said, his eyes straying back to the petition in his hand. "Harbor master," he murmured.

"Mr. Taft thought the job might get you to change your mind and stay," Alice said. "Could it?"

"Harbor master?" Tom half-chuckled. "They would never. Never ..." he muttered, his voice trailing off as he gazed at the petition. A smile slowly crept over his face. "Of course, if I did get the job," he said, "That really would be something. We'd have to stay."

Alice cried with joy as she and Mary rushed to hug Tom.

The City Council met to consider the appointment a week later. William Salsbury, the city's leading coal merchant, presented the petition on Tom's behalf, and read out the letters of recommendation. The panel heard the applications of the other candidates, none of whom had Tom's impressive backing. Then the vote came. One by one the councilmen cast their votes, and it soon became clear that the ancient incumbent was to be re-elected. Only a scattering of votes were cast for Tom. As Tom stalked dejectedly out of the chamber, Alderman Francis, whose victory

Tom had declared weeks earlier, hastened over.

"I'm sorry, Tom, really I am," Francis said. "I think the Republicans on the council—"

"I'm a Republican," Tom reminded him.

"I know you are," Francis replied. "I know you are. But after our embarrassment in the third ward-- your accidental election as warden, I mean-- I think we Republicans felt we had no choice but to vote as we did. Feelings in the city are pretty sore and if we elected you a second time, well, you know what they'd say."

"Oh yes, sir, I know," Tom replied.

"Maybe next year," Francis said, patting Tom on the shoulder as he took his leave.

There was a gentle grasp at Tom's elbow. It was Orray Taft.

"I am so disappointed, Tom," he said.

"Don't be, sir. I appreciate all that you and the other gentlemen did."

"Does this mean you'll be leaving for Liberia?"

"I reckon so, sir, this was a last throw of the dice."

"Is there anything I can do to change your mind about leaving? A foreman's job at the mill? Why don't you come by the factory this week?"

"That's awful kind of you, Mr. Taft, but I don't know the first thing about machinery. And your other men would kick at the idea of me being a boss anyway."

"Let them kick. When has that stopped you before?"

"I don't want to cause trouble for you, Mr. Taft. My mind is made up. Things in this country are not as they should be."

Taft grasped Tom's hand.

"If there is anything I can do ..." he began.

Tom shook his head, his eyes welling with tears.

"Well, good luck, Tom," Taft said. "Godspeed."

"Thank you, sir," Tom rasped in reply.

The slump of Tom's shoulders as he entered the house told Alice everything she needed to know. She rushed over to hug him, in tears.

Another packet had arrived and was waiting for Tom on the dining table. Tom opened the envelope, glanced briefly at the contents, and let them fall to the table.

"Read it," he said.

Alice picked up the sheaf of papers. It was the passport applications, returned in the mail. The attached note was neither signed nor dated, but read simply:

The applicant must certainly be aware that passports are not issued to persons of African extraction. Such persons are not deemed citizens of the United States. See the case of Dred Scott recently decided by the Supreme Court.

Little was heard from Tom Howland after the family left Providence for Liberia, without passports, three months later. Within months of their arrival in Africa, Alice and Mary had perished from fever, and Tom narrowly escaped the same fate. He recovered, however, and remarried, and for a decade afterward, at least, farmed a 750-acre plot on the St. Paul River, growing cotton, sugar cane, corn, and tobacco. No one in Providence ever learned what ultimately became of Black Tom, but in one of his last letters to reach the city, he vowed, with characteristic determination, to "win the horse or lose the saddle or die in trying".

The Anchor of the Soul
1774

On the third Saturday in June, slaves from all corners of King's County converged on the grove atop Tower Hill. Updikes came from the north, Babcocks and Watsons from the west, and Perrys, Robinsons, and Hazards from the south. Some trudged for miles with their shoes slung around their necks, putting them on only when they reached the contest ground.

The men who toiled on the thousand-acre farms of the Narragansett Planters alternately fried or froze with the change of the seasons. They plowed and harvested; tended dairy herds, fine horses, and flocks of sheep; mucked out the stables and privy pits; cleared land; dug up boulders; baled hay; kept bees; constructed outbuildings; shingled and roofed; chopped firewood; and built fences. The women spent their days tending crops; feeding animals; milking; churning butter; butchering; salting meat; spinning flax and wool; and making cheese, preserves, soap, and candles, among other things. Other slaves milled corn into cornmeal, and house slaves in the planters' princely mansions scrubbed, cooked, baked, laundered, and served the family's needs. All worked from sunrise to sundown, six days a week, twelve months a year, decade after decade of their lives.

Parmenteering Day, or the annual election of a ceremonial

slave governor, was anticipated by the slaves of the county with a mixture of excitement and dread. In the weeks leading up to the poll, the candidates' supporters canvassed for votes by means of persuasion, cajolery, and threats. The slave owners, coveting the prestige of owning the winner, joined in the competition, lending their slaves horses, carriages, and finery for the occasion, and supplying plentiful food and drink to keep the six hundred revelers in good humor.

The poll was conducted at twelve o'clock noon in a clearing at the center of the grove. There was last-minute jostling and bickering as men assembled behind the two contenders. The marshal walked along the queues with great solemnity, carefully counting heads. The counting complete, the marshal announced in a loud voice that John Hazard had been duly elected slave governor of King's County for 1774. The result aroused jubilation in the Hazard ranks, and gasps of disbelief from the supporters of Primus Robinson. John Hazard, a house slave disliked for his boasts of having "come up among the quality" defeated the Robinson man, whom his followers had been certain was a shoo-in. There was muttering that knuckle work would be needed to settle scores that evening.

The tarpaulins were pulled from the clambake pits at one o'clock, filling the grove with clouds of fragrant steam. A glistening bounty of quahogs, mussels, sweet potatoes, and vermilion crabs tumbled from cheesecloth parcels. Men and women scooped the delicacies up in their kerchiefs and shirttails as fast as the gauze sacks could be opened and sat in the shade of the trees to feast.

Their appetites sated, people dozed in the afternoon sunshine, while others played horseshoes or Blindman's Bluff. Men drank liberally from the barrels of sweet cider provided by Mr. Rowland Robinson. People thronged to the oak tree under which the soothsayer Sylvy Torrey sat, telling fortunes calculated to soothe fears or flatter fancies. Themillboy, the ancient miller, known by no other name, recounted, to anyone who would listen, the story of his arrival on a slave ship at "Point Judy" eons before. Jackrabbit Rodman, so named because his ears had been cropped for some misdemeanor as a youth, preached animatedly but incoherently, brandishing a Bible that he could not read.

Little ones were transfixed by Old Gamby's tales of Africa, a magical land where people built chimneys from the top down. Patting his "talking drum", the old man told how in his faraway home, cows gave such abundant milk that people made cheese in hollows in the ground.

Children ran screeching through the grove; women gossiped and eyed each other's costumes; men drank. The Robinson party's resentment smoldered. As the shadows lengthened, hilarity heightened and entertainments grew more raucous: Nancy Brown, née Joshua Hawkins, who, at the age of fourteen, had foresworn men's work and men's clothing, sang salacious ditties to roars of appreciation from the crowd.

People danced to gay tunes on Jack Noka's fiddle while drummers improvised, rapping sticks and shaking gourds. As darkness fell, the dancers pressed their bodies closer. Fires were laid. Some revelers fell asleep or collapsed in a stupor beneath the trees. Still more shouted boisterously, laughing and arguing with slurring tongues, their movements clumsy, the flickering flames and winking fireflies whirling before their eyes like a luminous hurricane.

No one quite knew what it was that ignited the powder keg: a smirk on one of the Hazards' faces, the suspicion of a mocking remark, or an innocent brush of the shoulders. All that anyone knew was that one moment Edward Robinson was placid and smiling, and the next, he lunged at Vincent Hazard with a murderous look in his eye. Sam Hazard leapt at once to his cousin's defense, attacking George Robinson, then Card Robinson throttled Bristol Hazard, and Cuff Hazard punched a bewildered Aaron Niles in the eye. A general brawl ensued, which the women enthusiastically joined. Experience Niles took vengeance for her yowling husband, yanking Beulah Hazard to the ground by the hair. Bethania Robinson bit Annie Hazard's ear. The Hazard's cook, Phyllis, swung a moonshine jug, striking Robert Brown on the head. Hercules, Cubit, and Joseph Robinson squared off with Moses, Henry, and Fortune Hazard, wrangling in the dirt in a writhing, snarling, howling, bloodied mass of tumbling fists and bodies.

As the alcohol-fueled fury spent itself, and the combatants' struggles subsided, they sprawled where they sat or had fallen to the ground. The groans of the wounded gradually subsided until the cacophony of crickets and peep toads filled the air, and the injured joined in the snores of the slumbering legions.

A sharp poke in the ribs awakened Scipio Robinson a little after dawn. Scipio, a strapping lad in his eighteenth summer, squinted grumpily up at his tormentor. It was Uncle Yella Ed. Scipio groaned. Yella Ed prodded him again with his foot.

"Hey, muttonhead," he hissed. "Let's go."

Scipio groaned again.

"G'way," he croaked. The youth's head throbbed like a clanging anvil. "I'm still drunk," Scipio moaned.

"Get up, boy," Yella Ed insisted. "We gotta go."

"Go where?" Scipio mumbled thickly. His mouth felt lined with flannel.

"Ferry," replied Yella Ed. "I got a p'mission note from Master Rowlan'. We got a dozen sheep to drive t' Newport."

"Newport?" Scipio moaned. The bleating of sheep all around woozily dawned on him. "I don't know nothin bout sheep," he said, turning over.

Yella Ed's boot dealt another sharp dig at Scipio's ribs.

"Ow!" the young man cried.

"There's a lotta things you don't know, boy," Yella Ed said. "I'm gonna learn ya. Now git yesself up."

Scipio sat up and rubbed his sore ribs, glowering at Yella Ed.

"We takin a wagon?" he asked.

"Wagon?" Ed snorted. "For sheep? You're usin shank's mare."

"Who's Shanks?"

"Aw, will you quit your foolishness?" Yella Ed said. "We got to be goin."

After draining a jug of water and retching and heaving for a spell, Scipio trudged along behind Yella Ed as he drove the sheep down the hill toward the glittering expanse of Narragansett Bay.

After an hour's walk, the men and their flock reached the South Ferry landing. A barge carried them the short distance to Conanicut Island, which they herded the sheep across to clamber aboard another ferry to carry them to Newport. Ed's old friend, Polydore Gardner, piloted the ferryboat, telling them of the ravenous sharks that patrolled Narragansett Bay. The man-eaters had developed such a taste for human flesh from devouring dead and dying Africans hurled into the sea, Polydore told them, that the sharks followed the slave ships all the way across the Atlantic Ocean.

Relieved to reach dry land, Scipio and Yella Ed drove the sheep on, their hooves clattering over the cobbled streets of Newport. Scipio goggled at the massive brick Colony House, majestic white church steeples, and whole rows of homes as fine as Mr. Robinson's. On the horizon, a forest of ship's masts jutted from the harbor. Everywhere Scipio looked, prosperous-looking people, white people, flocked to Sunday services, answering the call of the church bells. Such a dazzling place was straight out of one of Old Gamby's tall tales. And it was only a day's journey away!

Having delivered the sheep to the livestock pens, Uncle Yella Ed showed Scipio the stables where the Master had arranged for them to stay for the night. Ed had a lady friend to see, so he gave Scipio tuppence for his supper from the coin purse that Master had given him. With a stern admonition to stay out of trouble, Ed left Scipio to wander the streets of Newport.

The young man watched the white people promenading on Thames Street for a while and gaped at fancy goods in the shop windows. Standing by the Brick Market, Scipio spied two black men dressed like gentlemen in waistcoat and breeches. The elder of the two wore a dazzling gold brocade vest and brandished a stick topped with a brass knob. *He must be the slave governor of Newport!* Scipio thought. He hurried over.

"You the guv'ner?" Scipio gushed.

The stranger cast a withering eye over Scipio.

"What," he asked, "are you babbling about?"

"The guv'ner, you know, of the Newport parmenteerin?"

"No," the man sniffed.

"Then what you got up like that for?" Scipio asked.

"*Got up?*" The elegantly attired man scowled at Scipio. "Neptune," he said, addressing his companion, "This one is obviously a simpleton, but do you think he would do? He looks fit enough. Take him home and clean him up," he said.

The man glared again at Scipio.

"You're not a runaway, are you?" he asked, as if addressing a dullard.

"N-no, sir," Scipio stammered.

"Then you can help Neptune serve at my table," the man said. "In addition to that privilege, you will receive a hot meal. Neptune, set the table for six."

The man turned to Scipio again.

"You, bumpkin, mind what Neptune says, and you may learn something. Now, both of you, run along," he said, striding sedately off.

"Who's he?" Scipio asked Neptune.

"That's Caesar Lyndon," replied the young man. "Secretary to Mr. Josias Lyndon, a very important man."

Scipio was full of questions as the pair wended their way through the lanes. Neptune explained that Caesar was, like them, a slave, but a slave who could read and write and add figures and that that was what a secretary did. Such skilled men, he said, were permitted to work for money in the evenings and on Sunday afternoons, and often rented homes, as Caesar did. The supper at which the two of them would be serving that evening, Neptune explained, was in honor of Cuffy Easton, who was now a free man, having saved enough money to purchase his freedom.

Caesar's home was a modest cottage set in a little yard of fruit trees. A pig snuffled contentedly in a sty at the back. Caesar's wife, Sarah, was busy preparing supper as the two young men entered the kitchen. Scipio scrubbed with lye soap and was put to work singeing the bristles off the pigs' feet. Soon the trotters were sizzling and spitting on the hearth and a pot of stewed greens was bubbling away alongside them. Scipio put on the fresh shirt that Neptune gave him and was shown how to lay the pewterware on the table. The youths raised the window sashes to admit the evening breeze and lit citronella candles, bathing the room in a pleasant amber glow.

Caesar came home and his guests started arriving. Neptune and Scipio watched from the kitchen doorway.

"That's Zingo Stevens," Neptune told Scipio. "He carves the headstones in God's Little Acre."

A sharp-featured man wearing a gold earring was next to enter.

"He looks like an Indian," Scipio commented. "Who's he?"

"That's Cuffy Easton," Neptune replied. "He's half Indian. He's a draftsman."

"What's that mean?"

"Draws stuff they gonna build," Neptune said. "He's a free man now! And see them comin? That's Newport Gardner and his wife. He's famous in the town. A music teacher. Mmmm, bet that's Indian puddin Limas's brought. Betta go give em the wine," Neptune suggested.

Scipio carried the pitcher of currant wine in and stood dumbly among the guests, not knowing what to do.

"Where are the mugs, dolt, the mugs?" Caesar snapped. "This one really is slower than molasses in January! Set that down and fetch some mugs."

Scipio hurried to the kitchen to find mugs, his cheeks burning with embarrassment.

When, at length, Scipio had poured the wine, the guests raised their cups to Cuffy Easton's newfound freedom.

"To freedom," Caesar toasted. "Working all the hours that God gave you, my friend, has finally paid its reward."

Caesar gestured to the guests to be seated and bade Scipio and Neptune to bring out the food.

"Caesar says that we are all bound to be freed soon," Sarah said, taking her seat.

"The importation of slaves to the colony has been banned at last, thank God," Cuffy said.

"Praise be," agreed Newport. "And God willing, men of goodwill will help us to gain our freedom, too."

"More and more Africans are being brought from the farms to work in the town," Caesar said, unbuttoning the gold vest. "The manufactories are busy as anthills."

Neptune and Scipio laid glistening pigs' feet, roasted potatoes, and a steaming bowl of greens on the table. Newport led the party in grace, praying, as he always did, for the salvation of Africans everywhere. The guests all dined heartily, while Scipio and Neptune kept their wine mugs full, surreptitiously helping themselves when they could.

As the supper finished, Caesar, as was his habit, started telling stories from his youth.

"When I was a boy," he recounted, "My master, then a young man, came down from the college where he learned geography and history and other things. Now one spring, old Mr. Lyndon sent young Mr. Lyndon to Connecticut to buy cows. He was gone for two days. On the evening when he came back, young Mr. Lyndon told his father there weren't any cows to buy when he got there, so he'd bought a dozen goats instead."

The listeners chuckled.

"The young master's educated brain," Caesar continued, "figured that goats would do just as well for the dairy as cows, 'cause they eat less, and they give fat milk. We were all listening behind the door, laughing ourselves silly, when young Mr. Lyndon tells my Pa to turn the flock into the apple orchard for the night. Pa tried to argue with him, but young Mr. Lyndon wouldn't hear it. Now, in the morning, the old master was keen to see his new kind of cows, so he takes a stroll in the orchard. Not seeing any, he decided-- probably hoped-- that they'd hopped the wall and run off. But when he turned to come back, he heard a sound from up in the branches of the trees and what do you think he saw? His new dairy herd perched in the crooked limbs of those trees, looking down at him while munching all his apple blossoms."

Everyone roared with laughter. Neptune and Scipio cleared the table, returning a moment later with bowls and spoons and a jug of cream for Limas Gardner's Indian pudding. Dessert was greeted with coos of delight and disappeared swiftly.

Newport heaved a satisfied sigh as his spoon clattered into his empty bowl.

"As the day of our freedom approaches," he said, "education will be the key to the future of the African in America."

"You'll have a mountain to climb trying to teach the like of these," Caesar said, casting his eyes towards Scipio. "This one is ignorant as a goose."

"He's had no schooling," Newport said. "What is your name, boy?" he asked Scipio.

"Scipio, sir… Scipio Robinson."

"How do you do, Scipio? My name is Newport Gardner. Now, tell me, what is it that you do?"

Scipio's eyes darted from side to side. He hated being examined.

"Do?" he asked.

"Yes, what things do you do on the farm?"

"I… I lay stone walls, mostly," he answered, "Like my daddy."

Caesar chortled.

"Another chip off the old blockhead, like you, Zingo," he teased.

The wine had loosened Scipio's tongue.

"My daddy built stone walls could fence in the whole o' the South County," he answered hotly.

"I'll bet he has," Newport chuckled. "So, tell me, young Scipio, is there a skill to building walls?"

"Well sure… you gotta make sure they's wider at the bottom

than the top, so it don't topple over, and you gotta space the joints, don't line em up. And you gotta heart the wall real tight."

"Heart the wall?" asked Zingo.

"Yeah. You wedge big stones in good and tight with some flat little ones. Makes it nice and strong."

"You see?" Newport said, 'He's a bright enough lad. Just the sort of boy whose mind we need to cultivate. Teach boys a trade and give them religious and moral instruction."

"We need to form a *poro*," Zingo said. "I have said this before. Just like back home, where villages store grain for lean times, we should have a *poro* to look after money for peoples' needs, like education."

"A *poro*?" asked Limas.

"A sort of society to help one another," explained Zingo.

"We Akan have something similar," Newport said. "Sharing for the common good, providing aid to the needy, these are moral obligations for us. It is an excellent idea to start such a thing here, to oversee a fund to educate boys like this one."

"And look after the sick, and poor widows," Limas added.

"And to observe the burial rituals," Zingo said. "That is very important. The spirits of the dead will haunt you if they are not performed properly."

Newport frowned.

"We must leave behind superstition," he said.

"I think what Zingo means," Sarah said, "is the Yoruba saying, '*Lives must have a good beginning and a proper ending.*'"

"My granny says that!" Scipio exclaimed. "She come from Africa."

Caesar raised his eyebrows.

"If your granny is Yoruba, goose," he said, "you may not be as stupid as you look."

Even Scipio had to laugh at this.

"It is very important that this *poro*," Newport said, "should instruct people in the Christian faith. We must show ourselves to be good Christians if the English are to respect us. We will not gain it by drunkenness and gaming and frolicking, as the country people are wont to do."

"But we are different from the English," Sarah said. "We like to laugh and make noise and forget ourselves."

"It's true," agreed Caesar. "We hear drums in all things. It is our way. Are we forever to mimic the English and their constipated ways like you, Newport?"

Sarah tittered.

"Caesar Lyndon," Newport replied, "you are a maddening cuss. All I am saying is that our freedom will be hastened by virtuous conduct."

"Soon," Caesar prophesied, "Like Cuffy, I will have saved money enough to purchase my freedom and Sarah's. As a free man, I will do business for myself, keeping ledgers and brokering trades and drafting contracts for the important merchants. As more and more of us become free, you will see the natural resourcefulness of the African unchained. We are clever, we are resilient, we are hard-working. We will rise to the level of the English. The *Yoruba* among us, at least," he added, with a sideways glance at Newport.

This roused the Akan in Newport, but he checked himself, realizing that he was being goaded.

"Has it occurred to you, Caesar," Cuffy asked, "that the English will resent us for those qualities you speak of?"

"The English love only money," Caesar responded. "If Africans' exercise of their wits puts shillings in the Englishmen's pockets, they will not have a care about the color of our skins."

"But we do that for them now, and see how they mistreat us," countered Cuffy.

"As free men, they will not scorn us as they do now," Caesar said.

"What makes you think that?" Cuffy asked. "Things may get better for the likes of us, we can read, we have trades. There are two score African men of the town like us, but think of the hundreds of people on the farms, sunk down in ignorance."

"That is where the *poro* comes in," Newport said. "We must educate the country folk."

"When the country slaves are free, and can earn money," Zingo added, "all will contribute to the *poro*, and we will help them to buy land and build houses."

"And they will be free men, whose labor is sorely needed," said Caesar. "The English will be bound to respect us."

"But I am a free man now," Cuffy said, "and I am still an outcast, I suffer taunts and insults daily. We all do. We are made objects of fun if we are lucky, and worse if we are not."

"It is always worse for women," Sarah said, "They cannot abuse you men so easily as they do us. We are spat at, groped, almost every time we go out."

"And what of the laws and punishments that are imposed only on us?" Cuffy asked. "The curfew? Branding and lashing? I have heard no talk of these things going away. Will they disappear by magic?"

"These things, these punishments, they cannot long survive." insisted Caesar. "Like mud in troubled water, with our freedom, they will subside. We are Yoruba, remember? We overcome any obstacle."

Cuffy started to respond, but Newport cut him off.

"We must trust in God and be hopeful of a better future, Cuffy," Newport said. "The Scriptures tell us, '*hope we have as the anchor of the soul*': that must be our watchword."

"Amen," Limas murmured.

"Come," Caesar said, "let's be done with this wrangling. Let me tell you another story, about Old Cornelius, another of Mr. Lyndon's slaves. Cornelius had a grave manner and dispensed his wisdom freely. Now it happened that Old Cornelius was bird-dogging for the master one frosty morning, when Mr. Lyndon shot a fat loon. That bird fell out of the sky like a hundredweight of lead. Old Cornelius watched it come to the ground with a thud, and observed sagely, 'You might have saved your powder and shot, suh, 'cause a fall like that woulda killed the bird of itself.'"

Everybody laughed.

"When he'd come out with such things," Caesar said, chuckling, "the master never could figure out whether Old Cornelius was plain dumb, or a whole lot cleverer than he seemed."

The guests drifted away one by one shortly afterward and Caesar and Sarah went up to bed. Scipio and Neptune cleared the table, washed the plates and cutlery with a bucket of well-water, and extinguished all the candles. Neptune laid a blanket on the kitchen floor and the two young men settled down for the night. Crickets buzzed through the open windows.

Scipio's tipsy brain raced with the day's events. *Negroes with houses! Who dress like gentlemen! And own pigs! And give parties! Just as smart and fine-mannered as Mr. Rowland Robinson himself. And the things they talk about!* All of it was beyond Scipio's wildest imagination before today.

"Neptune," Scipio asked, "there many men like Caesar and Cuffy and them here?"

"Yeah," Neptune yawned, "couple dozen, I guess."

"You reckon they's as smart as white men?"

"Smarter'n most, I reckon," Neptune sighed.

"I reckon so, too," Scipio said. "Neptune?" he asked.

Neptune grunted.

"You think they gonna free us like they say?"

"Caesar seem to think so," Neptune mumbled.

A smile spread across Scipio's face as he lay in the dark.

"I never thought about bein' free," he said. "I think they's right, I think things is gonna get better for us."

"Hope so," Neptune muttered wearily, turning over.

Freedom! The word resonated like a bell in Scipio's head. He had never even thought about freedom before, but now, he suddenly craved it, ached for it. As he drifted off to sleep, Scipio knew in his heart that after the day's astounding events, he would never be the same again.

Devil Men

1730

Lamin swooned as he was forced down into the dark, stifling cauldron of the vessel's hold. The stench staggered him like a blow to the head. A dizzy kaleidoscope of sensations seared his memory: the cries of children; moans of the sick; scores of silent, imploring eyes following him from the shadows. A foul slurry of waste seemed to ooze from everywhere, covering everything that he touched and smearing his skin. Iron lacerated his ankle as men chained him to the deck. Convulsions of disgust and disbelief racked Lamin's being. He was covered in filth. His mouth tasted of it. Waves of terror flooded his mind as he confronted his incomprehensible, ghastly reality. He sobbed uncontrollably, straining in impotent rage at the iron around his bloodied ankle, until exhaustion robbed him of consciousness.

Lamin dreamed of the blessed land that he had left weeks before but now seemed an eternity away. It was a land of green mountains and lush forests, a place of warm sunshine and gentle rains. Forest spirits provided abundant fruits of every description, and the river gods filled the tumbling streams with fish. So dependable was the sunshine and fertility of the soil that yams and cassava could be harvested the year round. Watched over by the benevolent spirits of the land, the men and women of Lamin's community cultivated or gathered all that they needed.

Lamin's kinfolk had retreated to thickets high in the hills to evade the raiders who roamed the lowlands. Bandits snatched people for purposes unknown. Some said that the marauding bands were cannibals; others insisted that their captives were killed, and their bones ground down for magical potions. Lamin's hillside community was harmonious and orderly. The men farmed, hunted, and harvested honey; women gathered fruits and medicines and practiced handcrafts. Elders gave offerings to the spirits, taught knowledge of the land to the children, and settled disputes. In the evenings, the encampment's fireside echoed with old men's tales and the lively voices of women in song.

Like his father, Lamin was a skilled tracker and hunter, having learned the fundamentals of the craft as a small boy: to be watchful, to move stealthily, and strike swiftly. He was his father's favorite of seven children and, people said, the cleverest. Lamin married Jeneba when he was seventeen and she fifteen. Jeneba was a shy, beautiful young woman who loved to dance and weave. When the afternoons grew uncomfortably hot, she and Lamin would sometimes wander further up the mountainside where there were mists and cool breezes. There they would talk and Jeneba would sing to him until dusk. Lamin's life was one of hard work, simple pleasures, and ancient rhythms.

Not long after Lamin and Jeneba were married, a merchant came to the encampment laden with wares. The stranger, grown lame from walking, needed help to carry his sacks of precious ivory. He offered Lamin five grains of gold if he would carry his goods to a distant river. Jeneba pleaded with Lamin not to go, fearing that he would fall prey to bandits. Lamin insisted to Jeneba that their people could buy a cow with so much gold and reassured her that he would keep to the less-travelled tracks.

After two days' trek along the winding path, Lamin and the stranger descended to the bank of an expanse of water the likes of which Lamin had never seen. Many canoes drifted on the river's green-brown flood. The merchant assured Lamin that he would be paid when he had sold the ivory. They called on a fat trader who had a hut on the river's bank. The trader gave Lamin some palm wine as he haggled with the merchant in an unfamiliar tongue. Lamin must have fallen asleep, because the next thing he knew two bandits had seized him. He struggled woozily in an effort to escape, but the men bound his hands and feet with rushes. Lamin was bundled into a long canoe with several other men and women, and the kidnappers set off down the broad river with their human cargo.

A day's journey ended at a small island of sun-bleached shells. Fifty or so people were confined on the barren islet, guarded by bandits with firearms. On an island downriver in the distance, a great fortress of stone, larger than any structure Lamin had seen, rose from the palms. Beyond lay the distant, glittering sea. Lamin was stunned by its blue vastness. It was even larger than he had imagined from the tales that he had heard. The captives ate shelled fishes that they dug from the mud of the salty water each day. Everybody was desperately thirsty. Lamin could not understand how they could be surrounded by water and have so little to drink. The people greedily slurped moisture from the shelled fishes that they ate, and sucked dew each morning from the reeds growing at the river's edge.

Lamin became acquainted with his fellow captives during his weeks on the island of shells. Some he could understand with ease; others spoke in peculiar tongues. He took an orphan boy, Umaru, under his wing. The slender lad was thirteen, though he looked much younger. Issa and Kemokai were Mende from the hills upriver, not far from where Lamin came from. Ibrahim was a fisherman who, like young Umaru, was a Temne from the coast. Lamin also got to know some of the women: Hawa, Seray, and Simithy, a spirited, amply built woman. Simithy was an herbalist who knew powerful juju. Some of the people recounted that they had been abducted by bandits; others had been sold into bondage in punishment for supposed crimes.

One afternoon, a vessel with a tree-like mast sailed into the estuary. That evening, Lamin and the others huddled by a small fire, anxiously discussing their fate. What would happen to them? What was the mysterious vessel that had moored by the fortress?

"They are witches, come from a land of black magic," pronounced Seray, whom Lamin had decided was a rather foolish woman. "We will all be eaten!"

"Rubbish," replied Momoh, a merchant. "We are to be slaves."

"That's why they choose the strongest and healthiest of us," agreed Idris.

"Yes, if they meant to eat us, they would take the fattest and tastiest," teased Saidu, the *jeli*, or bard, to ironic snorts.

"They are rum men," Ibrahim insisted.

"Rum men?" asked Lamin.

"The rum men take people," said Ibrahim. "They have always taken people. Their ships sail to where the sea meets the sky, and the people are never seen again."

"It's true," agreed Momoh. "The chieftains trade people for rum and other things. They make war on one other to kidnap people to trade."

"But where do the rum men take the people?" Lamin asked.

"To their land to be their slaves," Momoh lamented. "A land from where no one can ever return."

"I have seen the rum men," Ibrahim said. "They are evil-looking creatures. They have no blood-- *mbakára*."

Lamin thought he had heard this word before. It meant white man, a mythical figure.

"They are soul snatchers!" cried Simithy.

"They are men," insisted Momoh.

"The rum men are demons, devil men," Lamin said. "Devil men who transport you to Hell."

Braziers glowed on the ramparts of the distant fortress, illuminating the skeletal silhouette of the devil men's vessel berthed in the river alongside it. Lamin shivered in foreboding. He hugged Umaru close to him in the cool of the evening and the two of them went to sleep.

In the morning, bandits came from downriver. Lamin and Umaru were bound and transported with several of the others to the fortress of stone. It was as they approached the grim structure that Lamin first saw them, standing on the deck of the tall-masted vessel. Devil men. They had the bloodless faces of cadavers and wore many clothes on their bodies. Their honking voices drifted ominously on the breeze.

The captives were herded into the fortress, to a large open pen holding scores of other people. There they were fed and given water to wash and fresh loincloths to wear. A pair of devil men chained the people and rubbed palm oil infused with spices into their skins. The men took evident pleasure in anointing the women's breasts with oil. The demon slickening Lamin's skin utterly revolted him. His breath stank of smoke, and the smell of his sweat was offensive. The devil men's skins were sickly pale like a white piglet's belly, and perspiration trickled from the limp, greasy hair atop their heads. Lamin sucked his teeth contemptuously.

The prisoners were led, fragrant and glistening, to a courtyard. There, a young devil man with a three-cornered headdress inspected them. Lamin took this to be the demon king. One by one the chieftain examined the people, and if the young king was satisfied, the person was led away. Umaru was among the first to be selected. The man loitered longer over the women, kneading their breasts with pleasure and feeling between their legs as the women protested. It was an outrage! As the devil chieftain arrived to inspect him, Lamin looked the man narrowly in the eyes. He smelled of shit and sweated excessively. Lamin swore as the demon prised his mouth open to examine his teeth. The devil king grunted and Lamin, too, was unchained and led away.

Lamin and the twenty or so others whom the chieftain had chosen were rowed toward the ship moored in the river. The vessel's stench reached Lamin's nostrils before they left the shore. It was worse, much worse than a pigsty on a humid day. It dawned on Lamin that the smell was human waste. *No wonder the devil king smelled of shit!* Then he heard the muffled wails of women within the wooden hull. *What,* he thought, *were these devils doing to people?* The boat drew alongside the vessel, and the devil men forced Lamin and the others to clamber aboard the Hell-ship.

The dream-vision of memory suddenly vanished and Lamin woke with a start. Disoriented, he realized that he had fallen asleep, chained in the disgusting hold. Blue sky shone through the hatch above. A devil man came down and exchanged Lamin's leg irons for handcuffs. He led him up the ladder onto the deck. It was late afternoon. The sight of home so tantalizingly close all but broke Lamin's heart, but it was a relief to breathe fresh air. Lamin wished that he could fill his chest with enough to last the night. It was refreshing, too, to be doused with a bucket of sea water, even if it did sting the torn flesh of his ankle. To be momentarily free of the slimy film of waste made Lamin feel human again.

A bucket of mashed yams, made palatable by a sauce of pepper and palm oil, was placed before the group of fifteen people brought up from below. The men waited while women fed handfuls of the gruel to the children, before joining them in hungrily devouring the food. Lamin refused to eat. The devil men berated him and started to beat him.

"Sons of whores!" Lamin shouted at them, "I'll kill you when I get the chance!"

The devil chieftain came with a glowing lump of charcoal in a shovel. Two men pinned Lamin to the deck while the demon held the hot iron close to his lips. Lamin screamed in pain.

"They'll force you to swallow it if you don't eat!" one of the women warned.

Lamin grunted and wheezed in capitulation. He burned with rage as he ate the mush with trembling hands.

As he was led below, Lamin's senses were once again assaulted by the putrid atmosphere of the hold. Women sat behind an iron grate in the dimness of the shallow middle deck. They had room to sit up or squat, but none to stand or kneel. Prodded further down the ladder, Lamin reached the lower hold where the men were confined in even more airless and claustrophobic conditions. Sewage lapped in the hull beneath them. Lamin gasped desperately. The stench was suffocating. As the devil men chained him to the slimy, rough-hewn floor, Lamin vomited.

The poisonous miasma hung thickly in the blackness of the hold that evening. The people quietened. Mournful voices in the dark told their stories. Musa, a sickly man, to whom Lamin was chained, was a farmer from a land far to the north. He had been imprisoned on the vessel for forty days as the demons called at settlements along the coast. Many of the men were farmers, but others were fishermen, ironsmiths, potters, and weavers. A few were warriors captured in battle. Discussion turned to the fate that awaited them.

"The vessel is almost full of people," a deep voice intoned. "The rum men will be leaving soon."

"This filth... I can't stand it," sobbed a man in the darkness. "This is a fate worse than Hell."

"Have courage, brother," said another voice.

"Courage?" moaned the man. "To face this?"

"Where will they take us?" asked an anxious voice.

"To their land to be their slaves."

"What can we do?" Lamin asked.

"Do? Can you melt iron with your hands?" a reedy voice replied. "What can we do?"

"We could try to escape before we leave our land," Lamin suggested. "We have to do something to resist!"

"Resist?" another man laughed hollowly. "We are in chains of iron, brother. Have you not noticed?"

"We must find a way to get off our chains," Lamin insisted.

"Alas, we have no sorcerer among us," an unseen wit mocked. "Only that old penis-snatcher, Simithy!"

The darkness rippled with guffaws and a muffled cackle of laughter from the women.

"Even if we got off our chains, the rum men have weapons!" the weeping man complained.

"Firearms," added the reedy voice. "We would be as good as dead if we went against them."

"We are lying in our own shit, brother, we are choking on it," retorted Lamin. "We are as good as dead now."

"He's right," pronounced the deep voice. "They are seven men, and we are thirty."

"Thirty men or three hundred, what does it matter when we are powerless?" agreed the reedy voice.

"The *orpofo* do not think that we are powerless," interjected another man. "I worked for them at the fortress and understand some of their words. They are fearful of us."

"These devils may have tools of iron," Lamin said, "but they are not men of iron."

"What is your name, brother?" asked the deep voice from the darkness.

"Lamin, a farmer."

"I am Brima. A warrior."

"A warrior! What must we do?"

"For now? We watch our enemy, farmer Lamin," Brima said. "Learn his weaknesses… and be ready to seize our opportunity."

The monotony of captivity continued the following day. Lamin was chained in the vessel's hold for twenty-three hours out of twenty-four. His movements were restricted by a length of chain fastened to the deck joining him to the older man, Musa. Lamin spent the days dozing or sitting up to talk in the dim light that filtered through gaps in the planking. Twice a day he was brought up on deck to be fed with a group of the others. The relative freshness of the air and dousings with seawater were Lamin's only respite from misery. He could at least clean his face and rinse the foul taste from his mouth for a few minutes. He saw some of the women: Hawa, Astou, and the indomitable Simithy. He glimpsed young Umaru's eager face behind the iron grate each time he passed through the upper hold. Lamin did his best to smile and affect confidence.

On the third morning, Brima was among the captives aired with Lamin. He was a powerfully built man with a warrior's ritual scars on his cheeks. Though handcuffed, the two men embraced as best they could. Brima looked Lamin up and down.

"I am impressed, young farmer," the warrior smiled. "You will make a fine soldier."

The two men wolfed handfuls of the unpalatable mush.

Lamin nudged Brima.

"Look!" he said. "One of the devil men is sick."

Brima glanced at the man. His skin was turning yellow.

"An opportunity?" Lamin asked the warrior.

Brima nodded silently and touched his fist to Lamin's.

The pattern changed on the fourth day. The people were not fed that morning. Devil men bustled overhead. A scent of roasting meat mingled sickeningly in the hold's putrid atmosphere. At noon, men came below and ladled out palm wine to the people. Lamin, like most of the others, drank eagerly. The men's moods thus soothed, they were brought on deck all at once, in chains. To their delight, they found in the open air a roasted pig on a brazier, sweet yams, and rice. The men feasted lustily of the bounty and drank still more. There was much laughter. Then the devil men took them two by two to shave their heads. By this time, many of the men were too drunk to object. Lamin was one of the last to be shaved. When it was done, the devil men seized him by the arms and dragged him to the brazier. There they used a red-hot iron to sear the flesh of his hip. Lamin bellowed in agony. His cries struck fear into the other men. They yelled and struggled drunkenly as one by one they were branded with the hot iron and led below. The women howled fearfully, comprehending their fate. Later, the men listened to the cries of the women and children as they, too, were tortured at the brazier.

The people were again denied food the following morning. Men scurried and shouted overhead amid thuds and scrapings. Chains clattered and ropes padded the deck. The devil men chanted rhythmically as if to coordinate some strenuous effort.

The vessel started gently rocking on the waves. Lamin perceived that they were in motion, gliding through the water. Ropes continued to patter the deck and there was a whip of canvas as vessel's sails caught the breeze, pulling it through the waves. The ship gathered speed. A howl of anguish and despair rose as the people realized that they were headed for the open sea. They would never see their homeland again!

Lamin was brought up on deck for feeding early that evening. Idris and Hawa were there, wailing and beating their hands against their heads. Umaru was there, too, sobbing. Lamin embraced the boy and he, too, wept bitterly. His sweet Jeneba, his blessed land, everybody that he had ever known or loved was disappearing into the dusk.

Only Sahr, the man who had bemoaned his fate a few nights before, seemed to be at peace. He looked composed and serene. Then he issued a strange yowl, almost like the mewling of a baby, and ran to the vessel's side. Sahr pitched himself headfirst into the sea and disappeared beneath the waves, making no effort to save himself. There was great consternation among the devil men at his loss, and the other captives were hastily bundled below.

The people were subdued that night. Desolation reigned below decks. It was much colder.

"Sahr was right. We truly are dead men now," a voice moaned from the blackness. It sounded like Lansana.

"If we despair, we *are* dead," Lamin said. "I mourn for Sahr—I saw him die—but we should not think about following him."

"Take heart, brothers," encouraged Brima's deep tones. "The rum men are getting sick! A second one is turning yellow."

"We are sickening, too," Lansana said. "Musa is getting worse, and so are some of the children."

"With every one of those demons that falls ill, the odds improve for us," Brima replied.

"Our chains disagree with you, warrior," countered a doubtful voice.

"And what about their weapons?" added another. Lamin

discerned the reedy intonation of Foday, a haughty merchant.

"If six men fall to the rum men's firearms, we have thirty more to finish the job." growled Brima.

"The warrior commands his army in chains!" taunted Foday.

"You mock me, brother, but I am ready to die for you."

"You will not die for me, brother," Foday replied, "any more than I will sprout wings and fly away from here. We are at sea, soldier. Can you sail a boat?"

"I can," a voice in the darkness answered. "I am Temne. I have been on the sea all my life."

"There are many fishermen among us," added Lamin.

"To pilot a vessel like this?" Foday scoffed.

"Stop your old woman's clucking, Foday," Brima said. "When the rum men come to take us above, they chain our wrists and free our legs."

"But they always chain our hands before they free our legs," reminded a voice in the darkness.

Brima continued.

"If I could attack the guard and get one of the iron tools--"

"The others would come and blow a hole in you," Foday jeered.

"And what of it, brother?" Brima demanded. "You want to live so you can serve these creatures?"

Men murmured in agreement.

"We must free ourselves," he continued, "or die trying."

"You speak for me, brother," said Lamin.

"And me," agreed another voice.

"Me, too," echoed a third.

Three nights passed. The seas grew heavier. The cold and the ceaseless motion of the vessel compounded the miseries of the people's imprisonment. Despondency deepened with each day at sea. Bad weather confined the captives in the noxious atmosphere below decks. Sores opened up on Lamin's back and buttocks. His body crawled with lice. Fever and diarrhea spread. Some of the men and women grew gravely ill and bled from their noses. Lamin worried about Umaru. The cries of children softened to whimpers and fell silent. The people listened to the splashes of lifeless bodies as the rum men tossed them overboard.

On the fourth night the swell grew even heavier. The deck pitched and shuddered as the ship rolled on the waves. Sick people groaned in the darkness. Men clutched at their chains to save themselves from sliding across the floor. Sewage sloshed up from the bilge and spilled over them. Rain lashed the deck. Urgent shouts came from above. The vessel wallowed in the heaving sea, its timbers creaking. All at once, a thunderous concussion shook the ship as it plowed headlong into a wave. Seawater poured in from above. Women howled in fear. Men were tossed about on their chains, splinters tearing their skins. Lamin tumbled to the length of his chain. He cried out in agony as iron incised his ankle. Musa moaned in distress. His leg had been pulled hard against the iron yoke in the floor when Lamin's weight pulled the chain taut. Through his pain, Lamin perceived that something seemed to give. He scrambled back across the deck. Fumbling in the dark, he located the iron loop fastening his and Musa's chains to the floor. The staples bolting it to the plank were loosening! Lamin guided Musa's hand to the loosening fixture and the older man chuckled weakly in comprehension.

The vessel lurched and heeled on the waves. Insistent shouts and clattering sounds came from above. The men clung desperately to their chains as the deck pitched wildly. Lamin braced himself against the iron loop and pulled hard at the chain. His ankle was bleeding. Musa mumbled encouragement despite the pain that Lamin's efforts were causing him. Once or twice the unexpected buffet of a wave sent Lamin tumbling painfully across the floor. He worked on and off for the rest of the night. At dawn, with wind and waves still lashing the vessel, Lamin tore strips from his cloth to dab the blood from the two men's ankles and dropped them through a crack in the planking.

"We must tell no one, uncle!" he whispered sternly to Musa.

Lamin fell asleep, exhausted from his labors.

As the storm abated in the afternoon, Lamin was brought up

for feeding in a miserable, cold drizzle. The demons doused Lamin and the others with buckets of frigid sea water. The saltwater burned Lamin's lacerated ankle like fire. The sight of the endless, heaving sea sickened his heart, though he put on a brave face for Umaru's sake. The boy had little to say and was dull and listless. Lamin feared that he was getting sick. The people ate hurriedly in the cold. Lamin observed that two of the rum men lay sick in a hut on the deck. The young demon king looked agitated.

When the sounds of the rum men had stilled after nightfall, Lamin confided in the others.

"In the storm last night," he whispered, "my chain started coming loose from the planks."

The men's chains rattled as they stirred excitedly.

"No! No!" Lamin hissed into the blackness. "We have only one chance. I think I can free myself and Musa. We can attack the demons with our chains."

"Musa is sick," said Issa. "He can barely climb the ladder."

Lamin's mind raced.

"I think I can get us free!" he insisted. "You must all stay absolutely still."

"The gods be with you, farmer Lamin," Brima said quietly.

The deck pitched gently on the rolling sea. Working as silently as his bonds permitted, Lamin resumed tugging at the iron yoke. He strained against the chain with the motion of the waves. He was in agony from the effort. From Musa's gasps he could tell that the sick man was suffering, too. The men listened to his work in the darkness. Someone sucked his teeth when the watch changed on deck, and Lamin remained motionless for a long time. His fingers probed the yoke's iron fastenings. There was no doubt that the staples were loosening. Half an hour after the last movement was heard on deck, Lamin resumed work. He heaved mightily against the chain. It was giving. He tugged with all his might. The iron loop flew from its base with a splintering sound and landed on the deck with a clang. Lamin felt certain that the noise had given them away. He stayed perfectly still. Nothing stirred above.

The men all wanted to shout with joy, but they remained silent. Though still chained together, Lamin and Musa were free to move about the shallow deck.

His bloodied ankle aching, Lamin searched in the darkness for the iron clasps that had bolted the yoke to the planks. He examined the fragments. They felt similar to the iron implements that the rum men used to unlock the people's bonds. Lamin tried the iron fragment in the lock of his shackle. Manipulating the sliver of metal in the crude mechanism for a few moments, it released.

"I'm free!" Lamin whispered. An excited murmur spread among the men. Women stirred above.

"Shhh!" Lamin quietly admonished the others. His hands trembled as he twisted the tool in the lock of Musa's shackle until it, too, clicked open. The two men were unchained.

Lamin scrambled across the deck to Brima.

"You have done it, my brother!" Brima whispered, while Lamin got to work on his shackle. Lamin freed Brima, Quashie, and Issa in quick succession. Releasing Kofi, a carpenter, he gave him one of the iron fragments.

"Free the rest of the men!" he hissed.

Whispered entreaties came from every corner. Where all had been stillness moments before, half-a-dozen men were now creeping stealthily around in the darkness, aiding their fellows.

Brima bade Lamin and Quashie to follow him up to the middle deck. Lamin limped up the ladder. The warrior signaled to the women behind the screen to remain perfectly still. Brima climbed to the top of the ladder. He put his ear to the hatch above his head and listened. The only sound was the wind flapping in the sails. He gently pushed the hatch up. It lifted slightly.

Brima took a step down and turned to the two men.

"We will rush the watchmen while the rum men sleep," he whispered, gesturing to Quashie to go below.

"Spread the word," he said. "We use the chains as weapons. We must be silent!"

Fifteen men now moved freely in the blackness of the lower

hold, with Kofi releasing still more from their bonds. Quashie descended the ladder.

"We strike now, while the rum men sleep," he whispered. "Gather chains, as quietly as you can!"

Men stole silently up the ladder, cramming the passageway beneath the deck hatch with Lamin and Brima. More waited in readiness below. Quashie passed a chain to Brima, who wrapped half its length around his hand, leaving the rest dangling as a flail.

"We must fall upon them silently," Brima cautioned the men.

Lamin was breathing heavily. The warrior placed his free hand on his shoulder.

"You have done it, brother," he murmured, "Courage." Raising his fist in a signal to strike, Brima stepped up the ladder and carefully pushed open the hatch.

The Virtuous Trade

1770

The sea breeze from the open window of Aaron Lopez's room in the counting house threatened at any moment to stir a whirlwind of invoices, letters of credit, and bills of exchange. Lopez, the wealthiest merchant in Newport, adjusted his wire-framed spectacles to inspect the latest issue of the *Newport Mercury*. His eyes scanned the front page until they rested on a small advertisement, which read:

Wanted: a negro from sixteen to twenty-five, free from bad smell, strait limbed, active, healthy, good-tempered, honest, sober, quick at apprehension, and not used to run away.

A thin smile crept over Aaron Lopez's face. *Grand!* he thought. *I may soon be rid of that impertinent little devil, William.* Lopez scrawled a note for his clerk to reply to the advertiser.

Lopez set the newspaper aside and pored distractedly through the pile of papers cluttering his table. An elaborately inked bill of lading caught his eye. It read:

SHIPPED, by the grace of GOD, in good order, and well condition'd by Aaron Lopez & Compy. in and upon the good brig Cleopatra, whereof its master, under GOD, for this present voyage, Nathaniel Briggs, and by GOD's grace bound for the coast of AFRICA.

99 hogsheads & 20 barrels New England rum

16 hogsheads fresh water
3 hogsheads tobacco, 2 barrels, ditto.
6 barrels tar
2 barrels vinegar (for cleaning)
50 loaves sugar
2 barrels molasses
20 barrels cornmeal
30 crates candles
500 bunches onions
20 barrels salt beef; salt pork, ditto.
10 barrels salted mackerel
1 barrel dried peas
30 ea., sheep, turkeys, geese
20 ducks
And to GOD send the good brig to her desir'd port in safety.
AMEN. Dated in Newport, this 2nd day of July 1770, Nathaniel
BRIGGS.

Lopez turned to the attached accounting, his eyes steadily widening as they skimmed down to the floridly penned figure at the bottom: £868.

"Infamous!" Lopez spluttered, hastily rolling up the papers. *Briggs has completely lost his head*, he thought. The merchant threw on his coat and strode purposefully from the counting house.

The brisk activity that Aaron Lopez found outside on Newport's waterfront never failed to gladden his heart, a satisfaction fortified by the knowledge that much of it added to his wealth. Hordes of longshoremen loaded and unloaded the never-ending flotilla of merchantmen that glided in and out of the harbor. Blacksmiths forged red-hot iron, hammering it into tools, fastenings, and mountainous coils of chains. Oily smoke from the chandleries wafted amongst the workshops, mingling with a pungent tang of tar and sweet note of caramel from the distilleries. A clatter of shipwrights' mallets punctuated the rhythmic "heave-hos!" and rasping saws from the lumberyards. Still more men labored in the heat of the pottery kilns, the ropemakers' and coopers' workshops, and the stuffy, lint-filled sail lofts, fashioning innumerable barrels and earthenware jars, mile upon mile of rigging, and acres of sails to carry the town's hundred-strong merchant fleet across oceans.

In the vast red-brick warehouses, feral cats slinked between barrels of cornmeal and great wheels of Narragansett cheese. They prowled among crates of salted fish, iron implements, woolens, and spermaceti candles stacked to the rafters. The fattened guardians of Rhode Island's bounty dozed lazily on stacks of lumber and sacks of dried beans, their tails twitching irritably as vermin scuttled nearby. In the battle of cat versus rat, the felines of Newport's waterfront were hopelessly outnumbered.

Aaron Lopez's wharf was the most capacious of the town's fifteen private wharves. At its end lay berthed the one-hundred-and-fifty-ton brigantine *Cleopatra*, fresh from Bannister's yard. Sixty-three feet of keel and twenty-three by the beam, *Cleopatra*'s unladen hull sat high in the water. Lopez's newest square-rigger was of the latest design, with ten feet in her hold, and three feet ten inches of space between decks for her cargo of slaves. The brig's fresh-hewn decking still smelled of pine, and her paintwork gleamed from bowsprit to stern.

Lopez spied *Cleopatra*'s master, Nathaniel Briggs, supervising the lading of provisions as he approached.

"Briggs!" Lopez cried. "I would have words with you."

"Come aboard, sir," Briggs responded.

At the age of twenty-seven, Captain Nathaniel Briggs was a veteran of five slaving voyages for Lopez. His command the previous year had been dogged by misfortune, fever having claimed the lives of two in ten of his cargo of eighty slaves on the return journey from Africa. Despite losing hundreds of pounds on the venture, Aaron Lopez appointed Briggs to command *Cleopatra*'s maiden voyage. The expenses that the shipowner clenched in his hand as he mounted the gangway caused him to question his judgment.

"What is the meaning of this, Briggs?" Lopez demanded. "Eight hundred and sixty-eight pounds? Have you taken leave of your senses? Turkeys? Geese? Are you departing for the Guinea coast, or preparing Christmas dinner?"

"I have ordered barely adequate provisions for the journey," Briggs replied. "All save fifty pounds was spent on rum."

"A shilling and eightpence per gallon for rum?"

"There is little to be had in the town for want of molasses. What was I to do?"

"God willing, two of my vessels return from Nevis and Jamaica this week loaded with molasses. That should relieve the drought. You must make haste, Briggs. Every day that *Cleopatra* dallies here is a day she could be on the African coast catching black-birds! Ha, ha!"

"I have consulted the Widow Tefft," Briggs replied, "and she cannot warrant safe passage 'til the morning of Tuesday next."

"Next Tuesday? What nonsense. What does that female know apart from Indian charms and foul-smelling poultices? I shall never understand why sensible sea captains listen to the gibberings of horoscope casters."

"You, sir, know nothing of the devils and fetishes that the Africans' black arts can conjure up. They have doomed many a vessel. They were behind that business at Salem, you know. I will not depart a moment before the favorable time cast by Widow Tefft."

"Sea captains!" Lopez grumbled.

"Sea captains," countered Briggs, "risk life and limb. All you risk is your fat purse."

"Which will be a good deal thinner once you have done with it," Lopez complained. "Such profligacy with my money! I ask, was there ever a man so sorely tried? Do you know the capital required to underwrite a journey such as this? Of course you do not. I shall have paid out, Briggs, over three thousand pounds before *Cleopatra* even slips her moorings! I have had to arm her, furnish her with all manner of fetters and chains, and supply sidearms and powder for you and your men. You cannot begin to comprehend my costs. There remains insurance to be effected—the underwriter charges twenty per cent. *Twenty per cent* to indemnify me against the hazards of fire, piracy, jettisons, and, ah..." Lopez said, casting a reluctant eye towards the captain, "pilferage, abscondment by master or crew, and so forth."

Briggs bristled.

"You have nothing to fear on that account, sir," he said.

"No," Lopez replied hastily. "No, quite."

"Though I am unhappily burdened with a poor to middling crew."

"What is the matter with the men?"

"*Cleopatra* is like Noah's ark, with two of every sort—two sobers, two sots, two passables, two miserables. They are the best that could be had for the paltry wages that you permit me to offer."

"You forget, sir, that I will have to pay those wages for perhaps ten months. It is all very well for you captains. For you, profit is guaranteed."

"For those of us who survive the journey."

"I have only risk, expense, and worry," Lopez continued, "while all the while you draw a wage."

"A meagre wage."

"A *fair* wage which you draw for many months and collect the wages of the slave who accompanies you. And when, by God's grace, you return, you will receive five privilege slaves and four parts in one hundred commission. Plus, a commission on the ten thousand gallons of West Indies molasses you shall have in your hold! You, Briggs, at no risk to your purse, will see no less than three hundred pounds from this journey."

"And you, a clear profit of no less than fifteen hundred pounds. Or two thousand!"

"I am much put upon, I tell you, Briggs, much put upon," Lopez grumbled. "I will be impoverished by the time the excise man has picked over my bones. He levies a duty on rum traded on the Guinea coast. They shall see me in a pauper's grave before they are finished. Do you know that this town remits forty thousand pounds to the Treasury in London each year? A large portion of it extracted from me! By the bye, Mrs. Briggs may thank me for preserving her skirts from spoilation."

"Eh?"

"For cobbling the streets! A tax of three pounds for that purpose is levied on each wooly head imported into the colony."

"I need not remind you, Briggs," Lopez added, "that your last journey incurred a grievous loss, one that I can ill afford. Another such would ruin me. No, Briggs, if you fail me again, I shall abandon the Guinea trade."

Briggs could not contain his mirth.

"You! An Ethiopian could as soon change his skin, sir, as you could be induced to leave so lucrative a trade," he chuckled.

"Fetch me the watchman!" Lopez cried. "Better still, the magistrate, so that I can swear an oath to the truth of the matter. I can make far safer money on the coastal trade," he insisted. "Trading candles for salt fish in Newfoundland, cheese for tobacco in the Carolinas, or sheep and horses for molasses in the West Indies. One can, of course, never lay one's hands on too much molasses for the distilleries. I could import iron from St Petersburg, silks and nankeens from Canton, or fine wares from London and Antwerp much more safely."

"It will be many months until I see a pennyworth's reward from a slaving voyage," complained Lopez. "The sugar planters purchase on credit, and it will be years before I am fully paid. The anxiety half kills me."

"But you profit mightily from the interest. Surely, that is the genius of your race?"

"Credit is merely the instrument of inducing a man to purchase today what he would otherwise put off until tomorrow," Lopez responded. "No, Briggs, my genius was to comprehend that every inch of soil in the West Indies can be so profitably employed growing cane that the planters can spare *not a sod* for raising crops or grazing livestock. I saw that the produce of the Narragansett plantations could supply the entirety of their requisites if I had the means of transporting their bounty thither. Look around you Briggs, look at the industry, the activity," Lopez exulted, with a boastful sweep of his arm. "Never in human history do I believe has an enterprise spread prosperity so widely. The vessels you see before you are the lifeline of those far off islands; yonder farms across the bay, their larder."

"Thus," Lopez proclaimed, "is the famous triangle of the Guinea trade made square, and its virtue, as a public good, perfected. As the estimable honeybee tends her queen, so God has blessed this colony with the means of sustaining the wellspring of its prosperity, the sugar plantations of the West Indies."

Lopez shook off the moment of grandiose reverie and resumed his high-handed tone.

"Now," he enjoined Briggs, "after the melancholy fate of your last journey, I want no shilly-shallying when you reach the African coast. Make straight for Anomabu on the Gold Coast and trade only with the Company of Merchants there," Lopez said.

"I shall make my trade with whomever it is most expedient to do so," Briggs replied. "If I find rum abundant at the Castle or slaves few in number, I shall have to lie off the coast for weeks or make for Elmina or Fort Christiansborg."

"And multiply the duties and factors' fees at each port you visit? No, Briggs, no. And pray, captain, pray, do not waste time piddling with blacks."

"I need no lessons in trading for negroes, sir," Briggs replied.

"Well, mind you do not dawdle there as you did last time. I cannot bear the thought of your lingering in the tropics while my beautiful ship rots beneath your feet. And we want no sickness to spread."

"No."

Lopez peered through his spectacles at Briggs.

"You had how many jettisons from *Hannah*?" he asked. "Eighteen, I believe?"

"I had no choice," retorted Briggs. "The dying would only have spread the sickness to the crew and the others. And what of it? You were insured for the losses."

"What of it, you say? Your disregard for my profit sorely troubles me, Briggs. Have you no compassion, sir? If you are careless of my profit, it will vanish utterly."

Lopez paused for a moment to take a pinch of snuff. He snuffled and gasped and gulped and sneezed forcefully.

"And another thing, Briggs," the merchant sniffed at length, wiping his nose with a handkerchief, "pray do not bring back so many *children* this time. Fully half of your last cargo were but waifs."

"Does it prick your conscience, Mr. Lopez?"

"Conscience? Why should it? Is not the prosperity of the town proof that the Almighty smiles upon our enterprise? Have I not heard that the elders of your church breathe a prayer of thanks when a slaver appears in the harbor, bearing as it does another cargo of souls to receive the Gospel dispensation?"

"So it is said."

"Why, then, should my conscience be troubled? No, sir, it is simply that it is not sound business. Children fetch a lower price," Lopez said, absent-mindedly tracing a finger over the gunwale. "Fetch me plenty of sturdy *bull* negroes," he purred.

"A mix of ages and sexes promotes good order. Especially with an inexperienced crew."

"And with this mix, as you call it, how will you keep order?"

"The negroes shall have feeding and airing twice a day," Briggs said, "and on Monday mornings they may have pipes and tobacco."

"Tobacco!" Lopez spluttered. "Am I to pay for the disport of savages?"

"If you want to keep them in good humor."

"I care nothing for their humor, Briggs, only that they should fetch a good price. Tobacco! You abuse me, sir."

"My anxieties will be eased only when we reach Surinam," the captain continued. "I will lay up there for two weeks to allow the blacks to recover from the voyage."

"Still more extravagance!" Lopez exclaimed. "Upon my word, was there ever a man so ill-treated as I? You really mustn't coddle negroes, Briggs. You will spoil them, utterly spoil them. In my acquaintance with blacks, they will wail and moan like pitiful children, but nine out of ten them have the *constitutions of oxen.*"

"The negroes fetch a better price when they are rested."

"You will only encourage their natural idleness, sir, if you dally to fatten them up. You will rob me of every penny of profit!"

"I shall increase your profit, sir, by resting the slaves in Surinam."

"I want no repeat of your last venture, Briggs."

"By the blessings of God, I will deliver a good cargo when we reach Barbados."

"And you will not depart until next Tuesday?"

"That is the first auspicious date," Briggs replied, adding, "You'll not find a master willing to sail without a horoscope, not to the Guinea coast."

"Confound it, Briggs, you will be the ruin of me," Lopez grumbled.

"It is in the hands of the Almighty, sir, whether we shall pick profit or reap calamity from this voyage."

Lopez pursed his lips as if sucking on a lemon.

"Tuesday it is," he said, extending his hand to the captain. "*Deo volente,*" he said. "May propitious Heaven bless your journey."

Briggs grasped the merchant's hand.

"Godspeed our enterprise, sir," he replied. "May we both profit handsomely."

Cleopatra set sail the following week. Ten days of storms on the outward journey strained the brigantine's hull, and seawater damaged much of the tobacco and cornmeal she was carrying. A gale was blowing on the fiftieth day of the voyage, when, at dusk, *Cleopatra* sighted Anomabu Castle. To the crew's dismay, another Newport vessel, *Dolphin,* was standing off the coast, but with night falling and the weather deteriorating, her master was evidently fearful of the treacherous reef that surrounded the fort. With great skill, Briggs navigated around the rocks and dropped anchor in their lee. As the gale intensified, *Cleopatra*'s crew lost sight of the rival vessel.

When morning came, there was no sign of *Dolphin* on the horizon; she had doubtless been driven far leeward by winds and storm currents. Briggs learned that the Castle had been raided by a local chieftain weeks earlier, and that the Company of Merchants were in desperate need of tobacco to trade. He called on the fort's governor, a man named Metcalfe. The air was thick with humidity in the governor's spacious chamber.

"My master was quite insistent, sir," Briggs dissimulated, "He will have me sell the whole of my cargo to one buyer only."

'The town is awash with rum," Metcalfe replied. "And with French brandy, too. Our only want is of tobacco."

"Alas, Mr. Aaron Lopez is a harsh master; his orders were quite specific. If you will not purchase my rum and dry goods together with the tobacco, I am to make for Fort Amsterdam to sell the cargo there."

"I am acquainted with Mr. Lopez by reputation," Metcalfe responded. "He is known for his plain dealing, and in my experience has been most accommodating."

"He may have been in a queer temper when I took my instructions, sir, but he was most adamant. I dare not defy him."

"So be it. The Dutchmen at Fort Amsterdam may have no want of your cargo; that is your affair. Our need for tobacco is not so great that we shall submit to extortion. We will bide our time until another vessel calls."

For three long days and three sleepless nights Briggs parried Metcalfe's blandishments to sell his tobacco, all the while expecting *Dolphin* to appear on the horizon. As the governor bade him to return to his chamber each day, though, the captain kept his nerve. On the morning of the fourth day, Briggs was summoned once again to Metcalfe's chamber.

"'Tis a fair wind blowing this morning, sir," Briggs told his host.

"As we cannot come to terms, I should be a fool not to take advantage of it. I have come to take my leave."

"I will raise my offer to twelve shillings per hundredweight of tobacco and purchase all of your cornmeal," Metcalfe said. "Your dry goods will find no market here. The blacks want no calicoes; they prefer their own garish cloth. Would that you had more tobacco, in place of such goods, I should take all of it."

Briggs sighed.

"'Tis a pity, sir, that I cannot discharge my master's command," Briggs said, bowing. "I bid you good day. Fare thee well."

Briggs turned as he reached the doorway.

"How strange that no other Guineaman has called these four long days," he said. "Still, your luck is bound to turn. I do hope that the vessel upon which you wait bears tobacco."

Briggs left the fort and trudged down the beach to where *Cleopatra*'s longboat tossed in the surf. As he was about to clamber aboard, a deputation from the Company of Merchants came hurrying along the sands.

"Good Captain Briggs," a breathless emissary exclaimed, 'Pray return, and parley with us again. Governor Metcalfe desires us to say we will purchase your cargo, all of it, and he begs you to return, that we might agree terms."

Briggs returned to the governor's chamber to find him in a much more conciliatory mood. *Cleopatra*'s master negotiated a very favorable agreement to trade the whole of her cargo for the ninety-six prime slaves confined in the Castle's dungeon, with the merchants to pay an additional eight hundred pounds in bills of exchange.

Within hours of *Cleopatra*'s cargo of slaves being loaded on board, *Dolphin* sailed into view. Her arrival occasioned Briggs some embarrassment, as her goods were invoiced at lower prices than those at which he had just sold his to the Company. Moreover, the captain knew that his cargo of tobacco was contaminated by seawater. As it happened, however, there was such a scramble among the African merchants when the hogsheads of tobacco were broken up that all of it was traded, save for two hundred pounds or so that was completely rotten.

Captain Nathaniel Briggs's steely brinkmanship at Anomabu Castle became the stuff of legend in Newport, making his reputation and his fortune. The coup earned him a tidy sum and made Aaron Lopez a small fortune. Briggs made a further five journeys to the African coast as master and underwrote ten more as a shipowner. The sale of the two thousand African men, women, and children whom Briggs transported to the New World by these means secured him ample capital, a splendid home in Tiverton, and the hand of the daughter of a wealthy merchant. Every Sunday, until his death at the age of sixty-four, Nathaniel Briggs knelt in prayer in the pew purchased at Holy Trinity Church, giving thanks for God's grace, by which he, a humble sea captain, had risen to the prestige and respectability of the merchant class.

The King of Snow Town
1876

Providence hummed with industrial prosperity as the Centennial celebrations approached. The city's mills and factories churned out everything from textiles to jewelry, locomotives to screws, and rubber goods to precision instruments. The sidewalks of downtown bustled with shoppers and thoroughfares were congested with horsecars. To the east, gleaming white church steeples sprouted from the green canopy of College Hill, under which the elegant homes of the scions of industry sheltered. Down on the waterfront, steam cranes chugged and clattered as they unloaded freighters and clippers, while dozens more vessels waited in the river to deliver their cargoes and carry the city's myriad manufactures to all corners of the world.

At the city's heart lay the Cove, a circular basin into which emptied the industrial effluents and human waste of the city and the towns upstream. Once a beauty spot for promenading, the Cove was now principally renowned for its olfactory aspect, which was particularly arresting in summer. On the sandy soil of the cesspit's northern shore, climbing up the rough ground of Smith Hill, nestled a community resignedly habituated to the Cove's relentless stink, a cheerless settlement of tumbledown houses, vacant lots, and desolation: the last place that anybody would choose to live. This was Snow Town.

Snow Town was a stone's throw from City Hall, but a hundred miles from Providence's affluent East Side. Hemmed in by the railroad tracks, the district's main thoroughfare, Gaspee Street, was bookended by the workhouse and the old State Prison. Snow Town's dusty lanes were scattered with dilapidated clapboard cottages, begrimed with age. Many of the structures had long-since ceased to be maintained, some collapsing into shattered heaps that residents quarried for firewood.

Rents were cheap in Snow Town, but steep for the people who lived there. At the better end of Gaspee Street stood a large gambrel-roofed boarding house, which housed many of Snow Town's Irish. The Irish tended to be new arrivals; they soon enough found better lodgings amongst their kin. There was, at best, uneasy tolerance between the Irish and Snow Town's majority black population. The blacks resented the Irish because they took scarce jobs; the Irish hated the blacks out of a craving for social superiority.

The structures grew ricketier and the faces of the inhabitants darker as one descended the slope of Gaspee Street. Stovepipes poked from sagging roofs. Few windows were unbroken; rags fluttered in the windows that were not boarded up. Not a single blade of grass grew in the dusty, refuse-strewn open spaces between the houses where the contents of dishpans, washbasins, and worse were emptied. Hens picked at the sand, and rats scurried from cellar to cellar.

The pretense of streets ended in sandy, unnamed tracks on the banks of the Cove. Amid the rotting pilings on its noxious shores were the most pitiful of Snow Town's lodgings; half-collapsed shacks offering bare shelter for the old, the sick, and the desperate. From such misery, there was only one escape, and the wretched seldom had long to wait. Everywhere one looked in Snow Town there was destitution and decay. Just about the only things the place had plenty of were sand, fleas, and shoeless urchins.

City newspapers complained of the idleness of Snow Town's poor, but the truth was that scorned as they were, some of the district's black inhabitants could find no work at all. So absolute was the hopelessness of these unfortunate individuals that they sometimes possessed a mule-like resistance to any constructive effort. Powerless against a succession of worsening crises that befell them, they often drowned their sorrows in rotgut liquor. These forlorn souls sat by the roadside all day, gazing at the world around them, gradually poisoning themselves, or losing their minds, or both.

For every man or woman who had given up hope, though, there were ten who toiled long hours for meager wages. The lucky men found work as janitors, gravediggers, ash collectors, barbers' helpers, or ragmen. Some watered the city streets to keep the dust down, while others rose at dawn each day to trudge four miles to Roger Williams Park, where for pennies they tended the pristine gardens enjoyed by the well-to-do. Many women cleaned houses or worked as laundresses or did ironing.

Despite the squalor and deprivation of the place, joy visited Snow Town for a few hours each Sunday. On the Sabbath, Snow Town's faithful would file up to the African Methodist Episcopal Church at the top of Gaspee Street. In between the preacher's exhortations and prayers, Mother Burgison, a five-foot-nothing spiritual dynamo and the nearest thing that Snow Town had to a matriarch, would lead the congregation in song, accompanied by drums, rattles, and tambourines. Mother sang God's praises mightily, singing not of the white people's wrathful God, but of a loving God, a God who put rainbows in the sky.

Everything was in motion as the worshippers sang: bodies swaying, hands clapping, feet tapping, fans fluttering. Often the faithful worked themselves into an ecstasy, uttering fervent cries of affirmation. Some convulsed from head to toe; one or more of the women might collapse from the sheer emotion of the moment.

The all-conquering rhythm drove the worshippers on, the chorus soaring to rapturous heights. The mighty sound of the peoples' voices filled the hall, thrilling them with an unaccustomed sense of power. The world beyond the church doors vanished. The worshippers rejoiced in in the presence of God, their souls nourished by His love for them. There was exultation, for they knew that they were among the justified. Faith, and the joy of Sunday worship sustained many people through the cruel hardship of their lives.

Survival for a very different set of Snow Town residents depended on the night, and on occupations sustained by the patronage of sailors: illicit liquor, prostitution, or robbery. Snow Town was notorious for its grog dens and disorderly houses. It was said to be busier at two in the morning than two in the afternoon. In the wee hours, the lanes echoed with the sounds of fiddling and raucous laughter, women's screams, drunken fights, and police whistles.

Enterprising men like Emory Turner ran bawdy houses. Emory would rent rooms in one of the houses for two dollars a week and install a harem of women and a fiddler. With the purchase of a few jugs from the rum wagon, his bawdy house would be in business, offering men liquor, music, dancing, and women. The disturbances that always ensued attracted the notice of the police, so after a week or two at one location, Emory would shut up shop and find a set of rooms elsewhere. He informed the sailors' boarding houses of his new location, with a gratuity to make sure that custom came his way, and paid barroom missionaries like O Latham to lure sailors from the waterfront bars.

Olmstead 'O' Latham was one of Snow Town's midnight vagabonds: a conman, pickpocket, and thief. Everybody in Snow Town knew that O Latham was a skunk, but O was a clever son of a bitch, too, with a rubber-soled resilience that people in the district could not help but admire. Thieving cuss he might be, and a swindler who would stoop even to stealing from Mother Burgison who brought him up, but O possessed a boundless audacity that his neighbors could only marvel at.

O had displayed a precocious talent for crime as a child. At the age of ten, he borrowed a jacket, stuck a ribbon in the lapel, and collected donations downtown for the Shelter for Colored

Children. The donations were, naturally, trousered for his own use. Growing to adulthood, O learned other wheezes, such as the art of persuading householders in the leafy neighborhoods that a magical charm that he would entrust to them could convert a five-dollar bill buried in the yard into a fabulous fortune overnight. Under cover of darkness, of course, O would return and dig up the cash.

O had once famously escaped from police custody by cramming his cheeks with brick dust from the wall of his cell. With his mouth full of the stuff, O let out a shriek and fell to the ground, his body convulsing and mouth foaming copiously with crimson fluid. The mortified jailers, white as sheets, carried him from the cell and laid him on a table. As one of the men was examining him, O suddenly opened his eyes wide and yanked the man's whiskers, causing him to howl in surprise and pain. In the commotion, O leapt up and dashed out of the station like a greased pig in a lightning storm.

People in Snow Town had been on the wrong end of a policeman's nightstick enough times to hold in high regard a man who could outfox the police as often as O Latham did. Stories of his exploits burnished O's fame and deepened the affection that people in Snow Town felt for him, even when he occasionally transgressed against them. "There's no flies on O," people liked to say, "only dead 'uns."

The Fourth of July 1876 dawned hot and sunny in Snow Town. O rose early, or early by his standards, at eleven o'clock. He stepped over the unconscious forms of the previous night's revelers on the floor of Emory Turner's rooms and emerged into the sunshine. Two of Emory's coterie, the dark, voluptuous Ernestine Olney and slender Hattie Weeden, whom O had dubbed Buttercup and Half-a-Bean, were finishing their morning toilette with a washcloth and a bucket of water.

"Buttercup," O said, beaming at her, "You got a face that could stop a clock."

Buttercup giggled, her brows slowly knitting as she thought the remark over.

"Is that good or bad?" she asked.

"That's good, that's good," O said. "When's you an' me goin out?"

Half-a-Bean chuckled mordantly.

"What ya gonna take her for?" she asked, "Wind puddin an' air sauce? What'd she want with a low-down stinker like you, anyway?"

The women laughed. The burly figure of Emory Turner appeared in the doorway.

"How's my girls today?" he greeted the pair. "The others still sleepin? Say, put on plenty a that nice per-fume I got for ya. A man likes a woman t' smell nice. We gonna be busy today, cuz O's gonna be bringin us plenty o' men, ain't ya, O?" he said, slapping O heartily on the back.

"Sure, Em'ry, sure," O mumbled.

"He's gonna be down on Water Street and over in India Point, bringin them sailors over. And you won't be gettin up to none a your hijinks, will ya, O? This is fixin to be the busiest day of the year. I rented this whole house. I got six girls workin, so I need men comin in. You gotta bring the fellas here."

"I'll bring em, Em'ry, I will," O nodded.

Half-a-Bean snorted.

"Butta woun't melt in his mouth, would it? You can bet he'll be up to his tricks again," she chortled. "City'll be so busy he won't be able to help hisself, poor thing, too many pockets t'pick."

Emory towered over O menacingly.

"You ain't got time for none a that today, ya hear me?" he warned. "You got one job today and that's to *bring in Johns*. I don't want none of your nonsense, else I'll break every bone in your body."

Emory turned and went back inside.

O glared at Half-a-Bean.

"Now why'd you go tellin him something like that for?" he demanded.

"Cuz it's true," Half-a-Bean laughed.

Buttercup shook her head.

"Mother Burgison say you gonna wind up in Hell 'less you change your ways, O," she tutted.

Half-a-Bean considered this.

"Maybe Hell woun't be so bad for you, O," she said. "'Least all your friends'll be there."

O stalked off down the lane, leaving the two women cackling.

Snow Town was preparing for Fourth of July celebrations. Paper chains hung from the doorframes and ragged flags stirred in the breeze. Pots of molasses and beans simmered on fires. Cornie Watson sat on an upturned bucket outside his shack, wearing his Civil War forage cap. He had tacked a newspaper portrait of Abraham Lincoln to the wall.

"How's it hangin, Cornie?" O greeted him.

"Mighty slack," Cornie replied.

O paused, thinking.

"Cornie," he asked, "why you got that picture of Pres'dent Lincoln there?"

Cornie snuffled and spat.

"He was a good man. He freed the slaves."

"You call this free?" O snorted, gesturing to their surroundings.

Cornie took offense at this.

"He was a good pres'dent," he said, "Done more for us'n anybody else."

"He did nothin for me, or anyone else round here, far as I can see."

This got Cornie's goat even worse.

"Well, I never," he spluttered. "May Pres'dent Lincoln's soul rest in peace. O Latham, you think you some kind of swell, but you just a goddam thief."

"Aw, don't believe everythin you hear, Cornie," O replied, patting him on the shoulder. "There's a lot here gets stole on my credit."

O headed downtown, where the Centennial celebrations were

in full swing. Buildings were draped in red, white, and blue bunting and fluttering strings of pennants crisscrossed the streets. Spectators in their hordes, twenty deep, lined the sidewalks, watching the parade of marchers, fife and drum bands, and floats depicting the pilgrim fathers, Washington and Lincoln, and the burning of HMS *Gaspee*. Confetti rained down from a hot air balloon floating high overhead. The streets echoed with a cacophony of snare drums, whistles, cheers and shouts, and the peals of church bells.

The crush of people promised rich pickings for a man of O's talents. Customers jammed the apothecary shops and ice cream saloons, seeking fruit ices and root beer. Taking advantage of the hubbub, O flimflammed several shopkeepers, and relieved spectators on Weybosset Street of billfolds, a pocket watch, and a pearl hatpin, adding to the collection of two coin purses, a pair of spectacles, and a tobacco pouch he had harvested from the unwary on Dorrance Street. The problem for O was that he just enjoyed his craft too much: the risk, the thrill, and the satisfaction of a clean getaway, on a day when there was so much opportunity was simply irresistible.

It was evening by the time it occurred to O that although he had accumulated a bulging assortment of articles and the astounding sum of seventeen dollars, he had delivered precisely zero Johns to Emory's bawdy house. He gulped, wincing at the thought of the hiding that he was in for. O bought a bag of clam cakes and ate them moodily as he pondered what to do.

Loitering among the drinkers spilling out of the Narragansett Oyster House, O spotted a sailor incautiously revealing a wad of bills when buying a beer. The sailor was no more than twenty years old, drinking with three shipmates. O realized that the tipsy young man offered a way out of his predicament. For one thing, there was a chance to score four Johns for the price of one. O could take the young sailor and his friends to Emory's to have a chunk of their cash extracted, and O could grab what he could of the rest at his leisure. O sidled over and engaged the young man and his friends in conversation. He charmed the sailors with jokes and tall stories, and they were all soon firm friends.

"The fireworks'll be soon," O told them. "An' I know the best place in town to watch em. There's a house I know there, run by a friend of mine. It's a real good place. There'll be plenty of pretty girls and liquor."

The men needed no persuasion.

"Let's go," they slurred enthusiastically.

The five made their way to Exchange Place, where thousands of spectators were gathered to watch the evening's entertainments. The plaza was a dazzling riot of red, white, and blue under the brilliant blaze of the limelights. An orchestra played suspenseful music as a tightrope walker inched along a wire suspended high overhead. Onlookers gasped at every step and quiver of the acrobat's balancing bar.

O dragged the men, all goggling open-mouthed at the spectacle, through the dense throng and herded them across the railroad tracks to Snow Town.

Celebratory bonfires blazed in the lanes as O and the sailors arrived. Revelers were dancing to the banjo and squeezebox and feasting on baked oysters and beans. Jugs of rum and moonshine were shared with abandon.

O guided the men to Emory's place. A fiddler played in the front room, where dozens of people were dancing and drinking and laughing. Half-a-Bean sat smoking a clay pipe. O led the sailors over.

"Hey, Half-a-Bean, what you doin sittin' on the rent?" he teased.

Half-a-Bean grimaced.

"I'm resting," she groaned. "We are *earnin* our money today."

"Why you always gotta be so grumpy?" O asked. "Why can't you be more like Buttercup? Where is she, anyway?"

"Business," answered Half-a-Bean. "Who's your cute friend?" she asked, rising wearily to her feet.

"Name's Lester. He's a sailor."

"Is he now?" Half-a-Bean drawled. "Well, I never. Hi, Lester, you like dancin?"

The young man grinned stupidly. Half-a-Bean smiled and patted Lester's chest while muttering sideways to O.

"He got money?"

"'Course he got money," O hissed. "Mother Burgison didn't raise no dumb kids."

"Hey, Lester," Half-a-Bean purred to the sailor, "why don't you and me have a little dance? Emory's lookin' for you," she added to O in an undertone, as she led the unsteady sailor over to where people were dancing.

Sure enough, Emory Turner had spotted O and was making a beeline for him.

"Em!" O cried heartily.

Emory glared at O, grabbing him by the shoulders.

"Where the hell you been?" Emory demanded.

"Ow!" O exclaimed. "I been fishin! Just landed four guys."

"Four? These are your first of the day? You brought in four Johns in eight hours?"

"It's tough, man. I mean, guys was all watchin the parade an' the big show."

Emory patted O's bulging jacket pockets.

"I thought so," he said, "pockets like a general store."

"Em, brother—"

"Don't you Em brother me. It's the busiest day of the year, O, and I was countin on you! I've had girls sittin here doin nothin when they shoulda been workin. Now give me all that stuff, all of it, and get your thievin ass out there and *pull in some business.*"

A collective groan came from over where the partygoers were dancing, and everyone recoiled from Lester, who was vomiting on the floor. Half-a-Bean screamed.

"Goddammit O, get your friend outta here, get him outside!" she cried.

"That's what you brought in?" Emory roared. "A scrawny-assed kid? Get him outta here. You betta get out there and bring in some *men*, a whole lot of em, O Latham, you hear?"

O bundled the dribbling sailor outside and sat him down, propping him against the house. As Lester slumped insensibly to one side, O fished the roll of bills from his pocket. Unluckily for O, Patrolman Feeney rounded a corner just as O was crouched over Lester's supine form. The officer raced over and seized him. Startled, O rose to his feet swiftly and spun around, knocking the policeman off balance. Patrolman Feeney tumbled over, and O legged it like a jackrabbit. The officer blew his whistle for help.

Police whistles tooted in answer. O dashed down Chickenfoot Alley and swerved into Shoo-Fly Lane. He dived into George Batey's cellar grocery and hid behind a barrel as policemen rushed to the scene, drawn by Feeney's frantic whistles. Officers began pounding on doors with their sticks, and soon enough one burst into George's cellar, shining his lantern in the darkness. O leapt up and scrambled out a basement window, only to find himself emerging in full view of Patrolman Feeney. The burly officer chortled with delight as he strode over and yanked O to his feet. The policeman's panting colleagues soon joined him.

The commotion aroused the curiosity of Snow Town's residents, some of whom were drawn to the scene. A murmur of dismay spread among the crowd as they watched Patrolman Feeney handcuff O.

"I've been wanting to get my hands on you for a long time, you little weasel," Feeney snarled. "You're done for now."

Cornie Watson, still wearing his Civil War forage cap, stepped forward.

"Let him go," he appealed in a clear voice.

"Stay out of this, Watson," Patrolman Greene warned, "or you'll be—"

Greene ducked as loud whumps sounded from the vicinity of the Cove. Skyrockets whistled into the air and exploded in dazzling starbursts, illuminating the many faces in the crowd.

"Let him go," Cornie repeated.

"Keep your nose out of it, Watson," Patrolman Feeney barked.

"He done nothing wrong," Cornie insisted. "People's just enjoying themselves."

"He robbed that white boy," Feeney answered.

Another volley of rockets whizzed skyward.

Mother Burgison stepped alongside Cornie as the fireworks exploded with a flash and a bang.

"We don't want no trouble, Off'cer Feeney," Mother Burgison said, "but, ya see, people here's been celebratin Fourth o' July like everybody else, and we been havin' a good time today. We don't want no trouble, least of all with you, but we don't want nobody hurt, neither. And O here, well, he's one of our own, and we don't wanna see him hurt."

"He's a damned thief and you know it. Probably stole from every last one of you. Now, out of the way. We're running him in," Patrolman Feeney growled.

More thumps sounded in rapid succession as rockets streaked into the darkness. Bursts of red and white lit up the faces of the young men confronting the officers. A cascade of crackling sparkles glinted in a straight razor in one youth's hand.

As the policemen started to move, four youths stepped forward to block their way.

"Don't do nothing stupid," warned Greene, brandishing his nightstick.

More missiles shrieked skyward. Fireballs exploded in the air, their shimmering remnants drifting down.

"You got to let him go," Mother Burgison insisted. "Yeah," agreed a voice in the crowd. Dozens more murmured their concurrence.

"All of you just shoo," ordered a rattled-sounding Patrolman Greene, "or we'll haul in the lot of you."

A man laughed, and laughter became more general as the crowd realized the absurdity of the threat. Any fear that the people felt had evaporated.

"Get out!" someone at the back shouted. Others took up the demand, chanting, "Get out! Get out!"

The patrolmen ducked as a stone whizzed past them, then a bottle shattered at their feet. People began scouring the ground for stones or other weapons.

"No!" shouted Cornie. "We don't want nobody gettin hurt!"

"He's right," urged Mother Burgison, "We don't want nobody hurt, not O, not no policemen, neither."

The youths confronting the officers lurched forward, feinting an attack. The officers formed a defensive huddle, their nightsticks drawn.

Mother stepped forward to shield the policemen.

"We don't want no one hurt!" she cried. "Off'cer Feeney, can't you see? They ain't gonna let you take O. If you start blowin your whistles, it's really gonna start. Don't do it," she implored him. "For mercy's sake, not tonight, of all nights."

The colorful cannonade continued to light up the sky. Patrolman Feeney's eyes scanned the faces of the horde confronting the officers. Muttering a curse under his breath, he unlocked O's handcuffs, releasing him. Still shielded by Mother, Feeney and the other policemen retreated. Everybody roared with laughter as the patrolmen withdrew.

"We'll be back," Officer Greene hollered.

Buoyed by their victory, the people of Snow Town energetically resumed their celebrations. O hurried over to where Cornie and Mother stood.

"Thanks," he said.

"They'll be back lookin for you," Cornie warned. "Maybe even tonight. You gotta get away for a while, 'til things cool down."

"I got friends in Pawtucket," O said.

"Pawtucket ain't far enough," Cornie responded. "You want to git yourself someplace far away."

"Where?"

"Hmm. Scalloptown, maybe."

"Scalloptown?"

"Mmm-hmm. There's people I know there. South of here. Eas' Gren'ich. You can hop a train over at the freight yard."

"You got any money?" O asked.

Cornie glared at O.

"What d'you take me for, O Latham, a damn fool? You got the money you took off that boy, ain't ya?"

"Yeah," O confessed.

"That an' a lot more, I'll bet. The leopard don't change its spots, dud it? Well, you better git. Good luck, boy. You tell em I sent ya."

O was left alone with Mother, who folded him in a warm embrace.

"You was the naughtiest child I ever knew," she told him, "but ever since you was little, you had a spark a somethin in ya, somethin special." She uttered an invocation. "Get thee behind me, Slewfoot. You leave this one alone."

Mother kissed O on the forehead. "God bless you on your journey, son," she said.

"Thanks," O responded, as he set off trotting toward the train tracks.

"Repent your sins," she called after him, "Repent your sins and you shall receive the gift of the Holy Ghost. And, mercy, O Latham," she added, as O was swallowed up by the darkness, "no one never needed more repentin than you."

Little George

1730

Acrack of musket fire awakened captain's mate John Kilton and the four other men quartered in *Little George*'s cabin. Running feet scurried over the quarterdeck above their heads. Kilton scrambled for the pistol by his side.

"Muskets!" he cried.

William Potter sprang for the weapons chest. Heavy thuds and a scraping of chains sounded above the cabin. One of the watchmen, Wickham, cried out from on deck. Potter and Dickinson loaded weapons. Captain Scott, *Little George*'s youthful master, froze in panic. The boy, Jack, cowered on the cabin's floor. The pounding and rattling of chains overhead seemed to be coming from everywhere. Wickham screamed horribly.

Kilton rushed to the foot of the companionway. Through the open hatch above, a pair of Africans stood silhouetted against the night sky.

"Savages!" Kilton roared, blasting away with his pistol.

Both men were struck and fell to the deck. There was a cry and the splash of a man going overboard. Wickham shrieked in terror from the waves. Dickinson passed a musket to Kilton. Ebens, another of the watch, cried desperately for help. Kilton clambered up the ladder and let fly with his weapon from his perch at its top.

One of the Africans fell. Two others stood their ground, laughing defiantly. One had a blunderbuss. In the darkness, Kilton saw three more Africans dragging the struggling Ebens to the vessel's side. On the foredeck, a slave sat astride Doctor Harris' lifeless body, beating his head with chains. The slave with the blunderbuss levelled the weapon at Kilton. He tumbled back down the ladder as the weapon discharged, peppering the hatch's washboard with grapeshot.

Running footsteps pattered overhead. One of the slaves peered down the hatch. Potter fired his musket up at him. The attacker fell. There was another heavy splash as Ebens went over the side. He howled and spluttered. Many of the Africans were now gathered over the cabin, stamping the deck with their feet. They hooted victoriously. In the dim light, their powerfully built leader smiled in satisfaction at his captives below. He kicked the hatch cover over the scuttle.

Terrified, Kilton and the others reloaded their weapons in the darkness. Their young captain was still transfixed with fear. There were more celebratory shouts and rhythmic stomping on the quarterdeck above them. Chains were piled on the hatch. Every so often an angry kick landed against it.

"We're done for," Kilton breathed, in a tremulous whisper.

Little George was westward bound, five days out and one hundred leagues from the coast of Africa. Her master, twenty-four-year-old George Scott, was commanding his first voyage on a Guineaman, or slaver. On board were veteran seafarer John Kilton, first mate; Doctor Harris; crewmen Thomas Dickinson, Thomas Wickham, and William Potter; the cooper, Ebens; and the boy, Jack. The sloop departed Newport and reached Elmina on the West African coast after a seven-week outward journey. On arrival, Scott and his crew had the misfortune of finding two French Guineamen standing offshore. The French vessels had glutted the town with brandy and bought up all the local chieftains' prime slaves. After lying off Elmina for two weeks and being able to purchase only twenty-one slaves of inferior quality,

Kilton advised the captain to sail up the coast in search of better fortunes.

Little George called at Fort Orange and Apollona, but the crew found trading conditions there little better. Guineamen had called at both places days earlier, depleting the supply of slaves and depressing demand for rum. Seeking to outflank his competitors, Scott sailed up the Grain Coast in a wide westward arc, bypassing several ports and avoiding privateers. *Little George* made in for Cape Mesurado. Finding there a good supply of slaves, Scott arranged a lavish banquet. The local chieftains were feted and entertained, and the captain and his mate took care that the dignitaries were amply supplied with rum. The wheels of commerce thus lubricated-- and with their own rum well-diluted—the Newport men commenced trading. They got good prices for slaves: one hundred gallons of rum for prime males and eighty-five for females, and in a week acquired forty-three prime slaves. *Little George* sailed on to Frenchman's Bay and the fort at Bunce Island. The captain paid the customary thirty gallons "dash" to the factor and acquired a further thirty-one slaves, but the visit was curtailed when fever broke out on board. The fifty-two-foot sloop made a final call for victualling at the Banana Islands and set sail for the West Indies on the first day of June 1730 with ninety-five slaves on board.

Favorable winds and *Little George*'s small size enabled her to outrun a privateer that spotted her soon after she left the coast, and the sloop made good headway on her voyage west. Many slaves grew sick with fever. The children were particularly badly affected; six had been lost. Worryingly, two of the crew, Doctor Harris and Ebens, also came down with the sickness. By the fourth day of the journey, they were too ill for regular duty and the captain isolated them in a makeshift doghouse on the foredeck. Over Kilton's objections, Scott had posted the sick men to the night watch with Wickham so as not to overtax the rest of the crew. Recovering his nerve as the morning dawned, *Little George*'s young master cursed himself for making such a foolish mistake.

Women clapped and sang with the first light and children's footsteps tumbled overhead. The crew listened anxiously to the men on deck conversing excitedly.

"They're all out," Potter said.

The men on the quarterdeck above the cabin argued. Voices shouted over one another. Footsteps pattered toward the main deck. A block and tackle clattered as voices shouted from amidships. Dickinson climbed the companionway to spy out the shot holes in the washboard.

"What the devil are they doing?" Kilton wondered.

"They-- they're trying to turn her!" Dickinson gasped.

"They can't be," said Scott.

The Africans heaved laboriously in a coordinated effort. Ropes whizzed and splayed onto the deck. With a crack of her sheets, *Little George* came about in a smart starboard turn. The cabin was thrown into shadow as the sloop's new heading took her due east, into the rising sun.

Little George's motion faltered. The vessel shuddered as she drifted on the waves. The ship began to yaw, its bow falling and rising violently.

"She's caught aback. She'll ship water if they don't trim her," cried Kilton.

There were urgent shouts on deck as the Africans struggled with the unfamiliar vessel's sails. *Little George* tacked sharply to starboard and wind again filled her sails. The sloop steadied and picked up speed.

"These blacks may be fair weather sailors, but I don't fancy our chances in a storm," Kilton said.

"What are we going to do?" asked Dickinson.

"We must try to save ourselves," Scott replied.

"Keep your small arms loaded," Kilton warned. "But for them, we'd be dead men already."

Kilton took an inventory of their weaponry and provisions. They had four muskets, two pistols and a dagger. They had four jugs of water in the cabin, two of rum, a small sack of rice, a few hard tack biscuits, one keg and two bottles of gunpowder, and a bag of shot. The rest of the provisions were out of reach in the fore hold.

"The victuals won't last long," he told the men, "but thank God for the powder."

Late that afternoon, slaves gathered on the quarterdeck, rapping the boards with tools that they had armed themselves with. Dickinson and Potter poised with their muskets beneath the hatch, Potter halfway up the ladder and Dickinson at the bottom. The slaves pulled the chains from the hatch cover. They thudded on the cover repeatedly then pushed it aside. Potter fired. A man shrieked as the grapeshot found its mark. Dickinson took aim as Potter stood down. His musket blast caught several of the men. There were howls of pain and fury. The hatch cover was pushed back as the Africans stamped the deck in rage.

"Brutes!" Scott cried. "We'll have to put these savages down or we're dead men."

"Whatever we do, we'd best do it while they sleep," Kilton said. "Just as they caught us unawares," he added, glaring at the inexperienced captain.

"We have powder," Dickinson said. "We could make grenades with those bottles."

"There's twine for fuses," Potter added. "Those black devils would dance a merry jig if we sent one of those among them."

The Africans continued to hammer the deck with their feet.

"We might yet put them down," Scott said. "Let us get to work."

The commotion on deck gradually subsided as the crew prepared their bottle-bombs. As evening fell, Scott led the men in prayer that the Lord would bless their enterprise. The crew waited in silence.

A squall rose. Wind and rain lashed the deck. The slaves shouted and argued as they struggled to trim the sails. Canvas tore. The sloop heeled as she veered wildly first to port, then to starboard. *Little George* broached in the swell. Seawater spilled into the cabin as waves lapped over her side.

"The dullards!" Kilton cried. "She'll be over set if they don't strike the sails."

The sloop's motion steadied as the Africans struck the mainsail and turned her stern toward the waves. Scott's men waited in the darkness. Hours passed. Few sounds came from on deck. The Africans slept, the captain judged, sheltering from the storm. It was time. He signaled Dickinson, who sparked a firelighter, and Potter carefully ascended the ladder. The fuse of one of the bottles took light. Potter gently pushed open the hatch. One of the Africans cried out in alarm. An axe hurtled down the scuttle just as Dickinson passed the bomb to Potter. The bottle broke and the incendiary exploded, the concussion setting off the keg of gunpowder as well. The explosion raised the deck, blew out the windows, and threw everyone to the floor. The muskets all discharged their ammunition.

Kilton's ears rang as he recovered from momentary senselessness. His face was burned and his jacket shred to tatters. The cabin was filled with smoke. Rain fell through the open hatch. Dickinson lay moaning on the floor, badly cut and burned. The others were all peppered with shards of debris. Injured and exposed to attack as they were, Kilton knew that their situation was desperate.

"Jack," he croaked to the boy, "go up and parley with the savages."

The wide-eyed boy stared at him in bafflement.

"See if they will parley," Kilton gently urged.

"The boy?" Scott asked.

"They'll not harm him," Kilton hissed. "It will buy us time. There's a good boy, Jack," he urged the youngster. "I'll be at the bottom of the ladder."

Awakened by the blast, the Africans gathered curiously around the smoke pouring from the deck hatch. In the darkness, they were surprised to see the head of a boy emerge from the cabin.

"Please, sirs," Jack stammered, "my masters would parley with you, sirs."

The Africans' leader approached, towering over the boy. He peered down at the crew in the shadows below. He appeared to understand the meaning of the message but did not seem in a mood to negotiate. The large man waved the boy away and barked an order to his fellows. Kilton pulled Jack down the ladder.

"Well done," he told Jack, adding grimly, "This may be it."

Potter fumbled in the darkness.

"By damn," he whispered. "The other bottle! The other bottle of gunpowder wasn't broken."

"Thanks be to God," Scott exclaimed. "Load those weapons," he ordered the men. "Quick as you can."

The African men regrouped atop the quarterdeck, pounding it with makeshift weapons. They whooped and shouted, steeling themselves for an attack. Two men armed with hammers poked their heads down the hatch. Potter fired his musket, wounding both. An iron bar was hurled down, narrowly missing the wounded Dickinson. Scott fired at the attacker. He missed. The quarterdeck thundered over the crew's heads as the Africans stomped it in rage.

"Reload!" Scott ordered.

The Africans' leader shouted more commands. Footsteps padded above the cabin.

The damaged hatch cover slid back over the scuttle. A party of men noisily guarded the quarterdeck until dawn to discourage any efforts to escape. With daybreak, the African men decided to confine their former captors more securely, pushing a heavy object along the deck. They manhandled its weight over the hatch, trapping the crew below.

Fair winds carried *Little George* back towards Africa. Scott and his men languished in the cramped, stinking cabin for three days. They kept a careful watch on the slaves' activity on the main deck through the spyholes in the washboard. The Africans chattered and bickered unintelligibly. The crew collected rainwater that trickled down from the damaged quarterdeck. The problem was food. The biscuits had run out on the first day, leaving them only with raw rice, and their meager supply was rapidly being depleted. Twice Kilton, Scott, and Potter tried to shift the weight over the scuttle, but they could not lift it. With each attempt, the Africans hammered on the deck in warning.

On the third night of their confinement, there were sounds of exertion and a metallic scraping as a heavy object was dragged across the deck. Scott peered out into the darkness to see what the Africans were doing. A party of men were pushing a heavy weight across the main deck.

"A carriage gun!" the captain exclaimed. The carriage guns, as the men all knew, were formidable weapons, carried to defend against privateers. Such a gun could easily blast a bulkhead to pieces.

"They'll have found powder in the fore hold," Potter surmised.

"They won't know how to use it," Scott said.

"They're keeping the ship more or less in trim," Kilton countered. "I confess I'd not have credited them with that. Ready your weapons, men."

The Africans groaned and strained, hoisting the gun onto the quarterdeck over the cabin. Women chattered excitedly amid scraping sounds.

"Shelter in the corners!" Kilton ordered. He positioned himself at the bottom of the companionway, waiting for the hatch to be lifted. Men pushed the weight holding it down aside. The hatch slowly slid open, revealing the shadowy outline of a man aiming the carriage gun into the cabin. The fuse was lit. Kilton fired his pistol and dived for cover.

There was an almighty blast. Smoke filled the cabin. Bits of timber rained down on the crew. Miraculously, Kilton found himself unhurt. The others, emerging from the cabin's corners, were also untouched. Grapeshot had blown a section of the quarterdeck to pieces and embedded itself in the cabin's floor, but it entirely missed the sheltering men. The night sky glowed through the clearing smoke. Dozens of African men gaped down the newly opened hole in the deck.

Scott panicked and fired a musket. The Africans scattered, but some of the men held their ground. Among them was the sturdy, brash leader. Kilton raised his hand to his men.

"Hold your fire," he commanded. Looking up to address the Africans' leader, he called, "We must decide this matter, savage."

With a scornful laugh, the towering man hurled a canvas tarpaulin over the hole in reply. Heavy objects swiftly secured it in place. *Little George*'s crew were once again confined.

At dawn on the fourth day, Potter, on watch, sighted the distant African coast. People on deck sang and stamped their feet joyously. In the merriment, a cackling woman lifted the tarpaulin to empty a bucket of filth into the cabin. *Little George* heeled to starboard and sailed south. Taking bearings out the window, Kilton estimated that they were four leagues off the coast.

Joy turned to disappointment as the winds failed and the sloop was becalmed. The vessel made little progress in the days that followed. The Africans continued to harass their former captors. They hurled broken timbers into the cabin, and tipped buckets of seawater in, hoping to dampen the crew's gunpowder. Twice more parties of men attempted to storm the cabin but were dissuaded both times by gunfire. Captain Scott and his men were growing weak. The rice ran out on the fifth day after the revolt. Dickinson was faring the worst, but Scott had also come down with fever. Both lay on the cabin floor. Driven by hunger, the boy, Jack, contrived to clamber up on deck. The Africans put him in irons and displayed him to Scott and his men. The crew went two days without food. On the seventh day, a favorable wind returned and *Little George* at last drew nearer to the coast.

Kilton took another bearing.

"We are a half league off the coast," he told the men. "We must do something to force the negroes to come to terms."

"We could threaten to drown 'em," suggested Potter, who, with Kilton, was the fittest of the crew. "We could bore holes in the bottom."

"Aye," whispered the fever-stricken Scott. "They seem much

afeard of the water."

"Three feet or so of water will start her listing," Potter reckoned.

"No more than that," Kilton said. "We want a truce with the savages, not to put her on her side."

Kilton cut bungs and pried planks from the cabin floor, exposing the putrid sewage slopping in the bilge. Potter gagged as he waded into the greenish brown slurry to bore holes with an auger. Water surged in as the holes were cut. A slave below decks cried out in alarm as seawater unexpectedly gurgled up from below. The Africans rained debris down on the crew and stamped the deck furiously. *Little George* slowed and started to list.

"Hammer in the bungs," Kilton ordered.

The people on deck went quiet, as the blows of Potter's mallet reverberated through the vessel.

"You'll parley now, ye devils," Kilton shouted up to the captors, "or I'll drown the lot of you!"

"They will answer, by and by," he assured the men.

The Africans deliberated on the quarterdeck. Presently the canvas was drawn from the hatch, revealing the boy, Jack, standing on deck. He was still in chains. The burly leader standing beside him prodded him.

"I-- I think they mean to stand in for land and sail upriver—" the boy began, quaking with fear.

"River?" gasped Scott.

"Aye."

"The Sierra de Leon River?" asked an astonished Kilton. He gestured to Potter to check the port window.

"I don't know, sir," stammered Jack. "I don't think they want to harm us, sir. They mean to take her up the river and they'll go ashore and leave us."

"I'll be damned if it isn't the Serrilone River!" cried Potter. "They've navigated us back to where we started."

"There'll be Guineamen anchored in Frenchman's Bay who will aid us," Kilton said.

"I'd gamble on that sooner than capsizing her a half a league offshore," Potter added.

The captain looked up at the boy from where he lay.

"It's agreed," he rasped, "We'll not sink the vessel if they take her upriver and leave us."

The leader apprehended Scott's reply. He nodded solemnly and swept the tarpaulin back over the crew's heads.

Little George resumed her course towards land as darkness fell.

"Lunatics!" Kilton exclaimed. "Surely they'll not try to enter the river with night coming on?"

A little after midnight the vessel ran aground on a sand bar in the estuary. Her timbers cracked as the incoming tide battered her hull against the bar.

"She'll break apart!" Scott moaned. The rising tide soon swung the sloop's stern into the torrent, and she drifted up the river. The Africans struggled to regain control, but the ship's bow was holed, and her list increased. Half an hour later, there was another impact and a splintering sound as she ran broadside onto a bar. The crew listened anxiously to every creak and groan of the sloop's fractured timbers and prayed that she did split in two. By dawn, the tide had turned, and *Little George* was sitting in about four feet of water on a strip of sand not far from the river's north side.

"We'll not be taking this ship any further. If the savages have damaged the longboat, we've had it," Potter said.

"What will they do with the scent of home in their nostrils?" pondered Kilton. "Potter, ready your gun. You and I will man that portside window."

A large party of Africans, some carrying firearms, was gathering on the riverbank two hundred yards distant. A few of the men waded toward the vessel. The people on deck gabbled anxiously.

"Make sure they see your weapons," the captain urged weakly.

The men from shore approached, shouting up to the others on *Little George*'s deck. After a friendly initial exchange, it sounded to Kilton as if a dispute had broken out. He could not be sure, but it seemed as if the men from the shore wished to board the vessel, but the people on deck were trying to dissuade them from doing so. Kilton and Potter eyed the exchange nervously.

"Raise your weapon," Kilton ordered Potter. "Keep a bead on those natives and let them know it. It may be our only hope."

The tenor of the discussion between the Africans seemed to change again. The men in the water were beckoning those on the sloop to follow them to the shore. *Little George* rocked on her keel as one by one people went splashing over the side: first the children and women, then the men. They waded towards the shore.

The cabin suddenly blazed with daylight as Jack tugged back the canvas.

"They've gone," the boy cried. "They spared us. The men from shore wanted to board, but the slaves told them that you would shoot them."

"Quickly," Kilton exclaimed, clambering up what remained of the ladder. "Jack, help Dickinson and the master. The three of you gather up all the powder and shot you can. Potter, you and I will lower the boat."

Kilton surveyed the riverbank anxiously. More armed men were emerging from the forest. The women and children from *Little George* were nearing shore. The men waded not far behind.

"The natives have mustered thick on the shore," Kilton warned.

Little George's boat splashed heavily into the water as he and Potter freed it from its stays.

"Jack!" Kilton hollered, "You and Dickinson get in the water. You too, master. Give me those weapons and I'll pass them down to you once you're in the boat."

The men splashed into the shallow water.

Kilton scanned the river's edge. An angry din rose as the last of the men from *Little George* neared shore. An armed party was wading out. Scott and Jack scrambled into the boat and hauled in Dickinson. With Potter keeping a tight hold on the mooring line, Kilton carefully passed the muskets to Scott.

"Over the side, William," the first mate ordered Potter. As

Potter jumped, a musket shot whizzed over Kilton's head. He cast off the line and jumped into the chest-high water. Another gun discharged.

"Heads down!" Kilton cried, as grapeshot peppered *Little George*'s hull. The captain's mate took hold of the boat's bow and waded, guiding it toward the sloop's stern. A musket cracked at close range. The rowboat's gunwale exploded in splinters. Ricocheting shot pinged the water inches from Kilton's head. He ducked below the surface and pulled the boat around *Little George*'s stern. Sheltered on the sloop's starboard side, the men pulled the exhausted Kilton into the rowboat.

"Make for the other side of the river," he panted as he fell into the boat, "and keep the ship between us and the natives."

Muskets puffed ineffectually behind *Little George* as Potter rowed vigorously for the south side of the river. Still trembling from his ordeal, John Kilton took a last look at the stricken vessel, leaning on her side on the sandbar.

"Make for Frenchman's Bay," he ordered hoarsely.

The World Turned Upside Down

1783

The first sign of trouble that Scipio Robinson saw was the people, dozens of people, trudging along the Boston Post Road. They were mostly negroes, slaves from the farms of Kings County, heading north with their meager possessions on their backs. Among them were Ned Wilcox and his wife. Scipio called and hobbled over.

"Sip!" Ned greeted his friend. "You made it back, thank God! What's wrong with your leg? You been hurt?" he asked.

"Yeah, wounded. Where's ev'rybody goin, Ned?" Scipio asked.

"North. Ain't no work here no more, so we got to carry on til's we can stop somewhere."

"What? What about the farm?"

"Don't need us on the farms no more."

"What?" Scipio exclaimed. "Who's lookin after the animals, tendin the crops, layin the walls?"

"Planters don't need people no more," Ned replied. "They've been letting people go for a couple years. What Mr. Wilcox calls a d'pression. Ev'rybody in the same boat, near as I can see. Most of the people's been set free and let go. Hardly any of em left."

Scipio felt a knot form in the pit of his stomach.

"And Vi?" he asked, "Where's Vi?"

"Last I heard, she gone to the mill," Ned's wife, Molly,

answered.

"To Uncle Nat's?" he asked, "She still there?"

"Dunno," Molly replied mournfully. "Lord in heaven, the world's turned upside down!"

"Thanks, Ned, Molly," Scipio said, hurrying off. "I got to get to the mill, but I got to see Mr. Rowland first. Good luck to you."

Scipio's stiff-kneed gait carried him the half mile to the Robinson farm. The farm was deserted and the pastures overgrown. He walked around the farmhouse to the kitchen at the back. He called but no one answered.

Scipio hobbled around to the ornate front door and knocked. His cousin Flora, a housemaid, answered and coldly told him to wait. Scipio removed his infantryman's cap when his former master came to the door.

"G'day, Mr. Rowland," Scipio said.

"Do I know you?" Rowland Robinson demanded. "What business do you have coming to my door?"

"Corporal Scipio Robinson, sir."

Robinson squinted at Scipio.

"You were one of mine?" he asked.

"Yessir."

Robinson eyed the cap in Scipio's hand.

"You were in Colonel Greene's regiment?" he asked.

"Yessir. The 1st Rhode Island."

"I hear the colored soldiers did themselves proud at Turkey Hill," Rowland Robinson said, softening his tone.

"O, yessir. We fought them Hessians off three times while Gen'ral Sullivan's men retreated."

"D'you know how he was killed, the Colonel, I mean?"

"Yessir. I was with him at Pines Bridge. We was ambushed by Tory irreg'lars, attacked from two sides. Major Flagg got killed first, then they came after the Colonel. Them raiders had to climb over the bodies of eight colored soldiers to get him. We loved the Colonel," Scipio recounted, his eyes filling with tears. "Lord, they did some terrible things to that man's body. All because he led colored men into battle against em. 'Lot of our men got captured, but some of us 'scaped into the woods. They say the men they took's been sold as slaves agin in the Wes' Indies."

Robinson grunted.

"Well, there's no work here," he said. "There's scores of ex-soldiers, white and colored, roaming the countryside now. I have nothing to offer them."

"But sir," ventured Scipio, "you still got walls to build, and pigs to feed, and corn to shuck, that don't change, right?"

"You do not understand the *earthquake* that has happened. Lopez is gone. The other merchants have all gone, and half of Newport with them. We planters are all ruined. There is no market for our livestock anymore. Negroes are just idle mouths that we cannot afford to feed. You became a free man when you enlisted. Go and seek your fortunes elsewhere," Robinson said, starting to close the door.

"Sir, wait," Scipio said. "The truth is, Mr. Rowland, sir, I came for my bounty."

"Your bounty?"

"Yes, sir. You was given ten dollars to keep for me when I enlisted in the army."

"That money was in compensation for the loss of my property," Rowland Robinson insisted.

"No, sir," Scipio countered, "that money is mine, that was my enlistin bounty."

"What impudence!" Robinson exclaimed.

"It's *mine*, sir!" Scipio cried. "I fought for four years. You got no right to take my money!"

"No right? No right, you say? I'll fetch my gun and we'll see if I don't," Rowland Robinson stormed. "You are damned insolent. Get your moon face, flat nose, and wool off my land, or I will put a hole in your stinking hide! Now away with you!" he thundered, slamming the door.

Scipio shuffled away dejectedly along the bank of the Narrow River, to where his wife Violet's Uncle Nat tended the water mill.

Violet was husking corn outside the miller's cottage. She ran to Scipio as he she saw him approach.

"Scipio!" Violet cried. "Lord have mercy, you're alive! Oh, thank God you're back," she said, throwing her arms around him. "But you been hurt! I was so worried about you. If you didn't come back, I don't know what I'd do. Mr. Robinson let most of us go. There's people everywhere's got no work and nothin to eat. What's gonna become of us, Scipio?" she cried, hugging him tight. "Oh, thank God, thank God you're here."

Scipio's four-year-old son, Asa, peeped timidly from behind the cottage door.

"Asa!" Scipio cooed. "I see you!" He limped over and scooped the child up in his arms. The boy cried, not recognizing his father.

That evening, Scipio, Violet, Uncle Nat and Aunt Cissy ate a meager supper of jonnycakes fried in lard. Scipio recounted how Mr. Robinson had cheated him out of his enlistment bounty.

"I hope you didn't make no trouble," Uncle Nat said when Scipio had finished, "I don't want Mr. Rowlan' turfin' us out, too."

"I don't think so Nat, I cleared out soon as he said."

"Mr. Rowlan' been showing his true colors ever since the war, if y'know what I mean."

Scipio winced in pain and rubbed his foot.

"What happened to your foot?" asked Vi.

"Frostbite, last winter. We was sent out to attack a British fort. We marched all night, in terrible cold, on some snow-shoe things. But at dawn our Indian guides ran off. They tricked us. We was miles from where we wanted to be. A lot of us got frostbite and couldn't hardly walk no more. A few men stopped and froze to death. I lost three toes. I don't walk so good no more."

Uncle Nat held a sliver of wood to the fire to light his pipe.

"Times is bad," he drawled, "No two ways about it. White soldiers are comin' back, and colored men's gonna be left with nothin."

"People's headin north. I seen em," said Scipio.

"Where they goin?" asked Vi.

"Maybe Wickford," Scipio answered. "I been there once. Fishin village. Maybe there's work there."

"A lot of 'em's headin to Prov'dence," Nat said.

"There was men in the reg'ment from there. How far's that?" asked Scipio.

"Twenty-five, thirty miles, I reckon," replied Nat.

Scipio whistled.

"I hope we don't have to go as far as that," he said.

Scipio looked at Uncle Nat and Aunt Cissy. Both were looking thin and careworn.

"Thanks for lookin after Vi and Asa, Nat," Scipio said, "but we can't take charity from you no more. You ain't hardly got enough for yesselves. We got to make our own way."

"It ain't gonna be easy," he told Violet, grasping her hand, "'specially on Asa. It's a rough road, and we might have a long way to go. But tomorrow we're gonna head north like the rest."

In the morning, Aunt Cissy provisioned Scipio and Vi with jonnycakes, dried apples, and pemmican tied in a ragged shawl, and the family set off with Asa up the Post Road. Scipio and Vi wore boots, but little Asa had only a pair of ill-fitting wooden clogs to wear. He was soon crying in pain from the stony road, obliging one or the other of his parents to carry him most of the time. Rivers and streams that the family forded brought welcome relief to their sore feet. Other migrants, white and black, were, like them, trudging north.

The road traversed heavily wooded land, scattered with a few small farms. Scipio called at the first farmhouses that they passed to inquire about work, but sullen faces and slammed doors made it clear that others had already called on the same errand. A church bell was tolling the noon hour when Scipio and Vi spied a white steeple through a gap in the trees.

"I reckon that's Wickford," he told her.

The road took them along a tidy, tree-lined lane of clapboard homes. While Violet and Asa rested on a little village green overlooking a cove, Scipio wandered down a handsome row of houses toward the waterfront to look for work.

A riot of squawking gulls wheeled overhead as fisherman landed their catches at the pier. A clatter of mallets from a shipwright's yard echoed across the cove. Boats in various stages of construction or repair sat on props, while men hammered and planed and applied tar.

The boatbuilders stared at Scipio as he approached.

"Afternoon," Scipio greeted the foreman. "You got work for a laborer? I just got out of the 1st Rhode Island, an I'm lookin for work."

The man eyed Scipio skeptically.

"What kind of work d'you do?" he asked.

"I built walls on the Robinson farm, but..."

"Walls? Stone walls?"

"Yeah, I--"

"Don't need no stone walls at a boatyard."

The workmen snickered.

"Well, no," Scipio stammered, "but I done lots of other stuff."

"I bet you have, sonny boy," replied the foreman. "But why would I hire some ig'n'rent negro when I got white men, soldiers, looking for work? Nah, I got no work for a negro. 'Fact, you'll find we don't want 'em here at all."

The workmen laughed and resumed their work as Scipio withdrew, shuffling back to Vi and Asa.

"This place ain't for us," Scipio told Vi, reaching the green, "We gotta carry on."

"How much farther we gotta go?"

"I don't know, but we can't stop here," Scipio said. "We just gotta keep walkin."

The rock-strewn road entered dense woodland again. At each inlet and stream they crossed, the family paused to drink and soothe their blistered feet. The burden of carrying Asa all the time was worsening Scipio's lameness. After another two hours' walking, the woods thinned, giving way to farmland. A woman told them that they were on the outskirts of a town called East

Greenwich. Scipio was heartened by the news.

"There's men in the reg'ment came from Eas' Gren'ich," he told Vi, "they got colored folks here."

The road climbed a hill to a row of shops, taverns, and fine houses. The banter of workmen and steady thump of mallets drifted up from a boatyard on the cove below.

Vi and Asa waited on the steps of the town's splendid courthouse while Scipio limped down to the waterfront. Shellfish fragments crunched underfoot. The air was thick with the muddy stink of the sea. Scipio saw a few colored women digging clams in the mud while others sat on the steps of their weatherbeaten shacks. There were black men among the boatyard workers, too. They stared briefly at Scipio and carried on with their work.

"Hey, Aaron!" yelled one of the boatbuilders over the hammering, "another one of your cousins is here!"

Many of the workers laughed. The black men looked on stony-faced. Scipio did his best to conceal his lameness as he approached.

"Beggin your pardon, sir," he called to the boatyard foreman, "You in need of a carpenter?" After his cold reception in Wickford, Scipio decided to change tack.

"Another one," the foreman groaned. He climbed down from where he was working and ambled stiffly over.

"You really a carpenter, boy, or you just spinnin a yarn?"

"Sure, I been a carpenter. I can make all kinds of stuff… fences, and gates, and doors, and… well, stools."

"Whoa, whoa, son," the foreman said, "You think you're the first ne-gro with only the clothes you stood up in t'come here lookin for work?"

"No sir. You see, there was colored men from Eas' Gren'ich in the 1st Rhode Island reg'ment, sir, and when I seen those men there, I thought--"

"You seen em and you'd a mind to settle here, too," the man nodded. "No!" he snarled, poking his forefinger hard onto Scipio's breastbone. "You won't be stopping here. Oh, we seen the *parade* of ne-groes coming through, but we let em know that we don't want no spongers here. These fellas," he said, gesturing to the black men, "is our fellas, they're Scalloptown men. They cause no trouble and are no charge on the town. But we ain't gonna stand no idlers settling here, burdenin' the honest people."

"But--" Scipio started.

The foreman came nose to nose with Scipio. "I am *warning you out*, darkey," he growled, casting flecks of spittle into Scipio's face. "That means you wasn't born here, you got no claim to settle here, you got no right to stop here. You understand me, sonny?"

"Yessir," answered Scipio.

"Then on your way, coon!" the foreman spat.

Some of the boatyard workers laughed. The black men looked on silently. Scipio hobbled back up the hill, his cheeks burning with tears of rage.

"We gotta keep moving," he told Vi as he reached the courthouse steps.

"But whe---" asked Vi, "where are we gonna find someplace to stay?"

"We will, we will," Scipio assured her. "We jus gotta get outta this town."

The family trudged on as the road once again entered woodlands. After an hour, Scipio paused at a deserted clearing.

"We better stop before it gets dark," Scipio said. "The watchman'll lash us if he finds us out after curfew."

They found a grassy spot beside a little copse of trees. Violet spread the shawl and nestled Asa on it. Vi and Scipio took off their boots to relieve their sore feet and nibbled pemmican and dried fruit in darkness. Violet started to cry.

"What're we gonna do?" she sobbed. "White people don't want us round em. We got no place to go."

Scipio put his arm around her.

"We jus' gotta find a place where they's 'customed to us," he told her, "There's got to be a place. I mean, people musta gone somewhere."

Violet continued to weep.

"Hey," Scipio said, "What happened to that girl who'd chase anyone outta the kitchen who didn't belong there? Where's that child who'd put Master William over her knee if he caused any trouble?"

Violet chuckled through her tears.

"Well, would ya look at that," Scipio teased, tugging Vi's shoulder playfully. "Never seen no one could laugh and cry at the same time."

"I never thought we'd have to leave the farm," Violet sniffed. "We was all born there. None of us known nothin else. I'm just so scared."

"Hey… hey," Scipio reassured her, "It's gonna be alright. I seen some of the world, I know stuff. And we're free now! That's a good thing, ain't it? Things'll get better, you'll see. I'll find work. People still need walls buildin. Now hush with them tears. We're tired. Let's get some sleep."

Scipio snuggled Asa between him and Violet and gathered the shawl over the three of them. Soon they were fast asleep in the cool summer night.

Violet was up at dawn, picking berries. The family ate the meager harvest with the last of the jonnycakes. They resumed their trek north, following the coast of Narragansett Bay as it narrowed. Progress was slow on their raw, blistered feet. Asa was tired and hungry and fussing ceaselessly and had to be carried all the time. The family was passing mostly through farmland now as habitation grew denser. Hostile stares met them in each of the hamlets that they passed through.

"Black devils! You're not wanted here!" someone jeered in Shawomet. In Pawtuxet, children taunted them and threw stones.

In the afternoon it started to rain. The family plodded on through the downpour, drenched and exhausted. On the outskirts of a town, a tavernkeeper saw their bedraggled state and invited them to shelter in his stable. He brought them bread and butter and some honeycomb for Asa. The kind man told them that the town that they were nearing was Providence.

The family was awakened on the third day by wagons trundling along the rough road. Scipio and Vi thanked the innkeeper and they continued on into the town. It was soon clear that Providence was much larger place than the other settlements that they had passed through. Scores of dwellings, inns, and shops flanked the road. The town bustled with men on horseback and wagons laden with baskets, casks, and crates. Passersby hardly took notice of the family as they walked along.

"What a place!" Violet said. "Do you think they'll have us here?"

"I hope so. Don't know where else there is to go," replied Scipio.

The family marveled at the dozens of sailing vessels moored on the river as they crossed over a bridge into the market square. Carters ferried goods to and fro and stallholders hawked produce and wares to a horde of shoppers.

An old black man collecting manure in a wheelbarrow hastened over to them.

"You don't want t'stop here," he warned. "That's the whippin post. White boys make trouble for colored folk who stop here. Git yourselves to Hardscrabble, over that way. It ain't far," he said, indicating up the river.

Scipio, Violet, and Asa limped a few hundred yards along the riverbank to a shantytown reeking of rotting fish. Scores, hundreds of black people were camped in huts, makeshift tents, and lean-tos. More shacks dotted the slope of a nearby hill.

They found Aunt Mary Elizabeth Robinson sitting by a ragged tent pitched on the muddy ground. She greeted them warmly, as did several of the Babcock and Perry women whom they knew. To Scipio's delight, his old comrade from the 1st Rhode Island, Bristol Arnold, was in the camp. The former brothers-in-arms embraced heartily.

"You old scoundrel!" Scipio cried. "How'd you get here?"

"I got lost after Pines Bridge," replied Bristol.

"He means he deserted," Scipio explained to Vi.

"We got here last November," Bristol continued. "It was damn cold. I got t'gether some scrap wood and built a shack up in them woods there. So we didn't freeze in winter. I got work clearin land and been doin it ever since. It don't pay much, but it's steady."

"I see your legs ain't got no straighter," Scipio jibed. "Man'd be two inches taller if they straightened em," he told Vi.

"The way you's hobblin around, yours don't look so good no more," Bristol replied.

"These legs have carried me a lotta miles, brother."

"You used to build walls didn't ya?" Bristol asked. "They buildin some 'bankment jus up the river from here. You'll find work here, no problem."

"There other men from the reg'ment here?"

"Loads of em. Africa Burk, Dick Cozzens--"

"Dick? Wow. What about George Gamby?"

"George the giant?" Bristol smiled fondly. "No, Big George ain't here. They say he got tricked inta goin south an' got sold inta slav'ry again."

"What about them pensions? You think we'll get em?"

Bristol snorted.

"No man round here's got one. Colonel Olney say he's tryin for us, but you know no promise they make means nothin."

"And bounty land, was that jus talk, too?"

"Oh, there's bounty land all right. Only you gotta git yourself down to Penns'vania or Ohio to claim it."

Scipio sucked his teeth.

"You can't win for losin," he lamented. "What about all the land here? We seen practic'ly nothin but woods jus waitin to be cleared comin up here."

Bristol snorted again.

"No colored man's gonna get no hundred acres' o' bounty land round here," he grumbled.

Bristol guided Scipio and Violet up the hill to his shack where they could stay the night. Violet and Asa settled into the cramped quarters with Bristol's wife and children while the two men gathered firewood. As he foraged, Scipio spied a grizzled, dark-skinned man sitting by a lean-to deep in the brush. The man looked to be clad in little more than rags save for a gold waistcoat. Something about the odd garment registered in Scipio's memory. He picked his way through the thicket towards the man.

The stranger heard Scipio approaching.

"Who's there?" he asked.

As he reached the man, Scipio realized that he was blind or almost so. He had cataracts in both eyes. Scipio's gaze was fixed on the mud-spattered gold fabric of the vest. *I've seen that before*, he thought. Scipio searched the stranger's face, probing the features beneath the gray tangle of his beard. Recognition came in an instant. *Caesar! Caesar Lyndon!*

"Caesar!" Scipio cried. "What are you doing here?" Scipio embraced his old acquaintance, finding him to be almost skin and bones.

Caesar's clouded eyes struggled to see.

"Who's that?"

"It's Scipio Robinson. You remember, your supper party, all those years ago? The ign'rant goose?"

Bafflement on Caesar's face slowly creased into a toothless grin.

"Ha, ha! Goose. Yes, I remember you," he chuckled. "I was harsh in those days. Where have you come from?"

"I just got here. I was in the 1st Rhode Island."

"Ah, fine fellows. You showed them our mettle."

"What happened to you?" Scipio asked, "What are you doing here?"

"Alas, my friend, the British occupation brought everything to an end," Caesar explained. "The Master, along with all the other merchants, fled, and when he died a year or so later, I was let go. Soon I had not a pot to piss in. There's hardly an African left in Newport that does. I came here, hoping to find work as a scribe or a clerk, but no one here's ever heard of an educated African, much less wanted one. Now my eyes are so bad that I can barely work. If winter or the bloody flux does not carry me off, I shall beg my way back to Newport to wait for death there."

"But a man smart as you's gotta be able to find something,"

Scipio said.

Caesar shook his head.

"In Newport," he sighed, "men like Governor Lyndon and Captain Gardner understood that Africans were capable, that we had wits. Here we are all but dumb animals from the farms to them. I'm sorry, my boy, I'm sorry," Caesar said, his hand shakily groping for Scipio's arm. "I don't mean to wound you, but it's true. The white men here have swallowed whole the conviction that we are low and dirty creatures, and they scorn us absolutely."

"But the future…" Scipio ventured. "I mean… we're free men now. Like you and the others was sayin before the war, things'll get better now we're free, won't they?"

"Freedom," Caesar chuckled hollowly. "How we looked forward to freedom. But don't you see? We're not free, *they've just washed their hands of us*. The only freedom you've been given, son," Caesar said, "is freedom to starve."

The Stranger

1652

An anguished cry pierced the haze of woodsmoke hanging over the tiny settlement. Obadiah Holmes at once wedged his ax in the chopping block and hurried toward the sound of the commotion. Rain spattered his broad-brimmed hat as he squelched through the mud toward the hamlet's crude pier. Another whip-crack and terrible scream rent the stillness. The small crowd gathered at the dockside made way for Holmes as he approached. As pastor of the Baptist Church, Obadiah Holmes's authority in the settlement of Newport was second only to that of the magistrate.

Holmes stopped in his tracks, gaping in astonishment. On the dock before him was a man in chains, his back streaming with blood. The young stranger's skin was dark, and his hair was black and woolly.

"A blackamoor!" Holmes gasped.

The man's tormentor, Hugh Smith, delivered another fierce crack of the lash. The captive howled as flails tore at his lacerated flesh. He sobbed, begging for mercy in an unintelligible tongue.

Holmes was spellbound by the newcomer's strangeness.

"W-what is the meaning of this, Smith?" he stammered. "Dost thou think thou art a law unto thine own self?"

"What cheer, Pastor?" Smith greeted him, wiping sweat from his brow. "I do now learn this crafty knave his lesson. But scarcely had I taken possession of him, when straightaway he did flee. Men found him skulking in yonder skiff."

Holmes was transfixed by the sobbing stranger. The man's rain-slickened chest was heaving; his body trembled uncontrollably from shock and cold. Holmes looked on, gripped by an unwholesome fascination. A gnawing sense of dread grew.

"What didst thou think?" he asked Smith, "Hopest thou to enslave him, that he should not try to escape? Unchain the poor man."

"Nay, sir, I shall not. The lash is a harsh teacher, but he must learn obedience."

"These creatures be men with souls, Smith," Holmes reminded him.

"Pah!" Smith scoffed. "Blackamoors possess no more souls than cattle."

"But behold his form! Can we not recognize him as a man?"

"Man?" Smith asked. "To mine eyes, and, verily, to mine *nose*, he seems more a beast."

Snickers rippled among the spectators.

"The knave needs must be punished," Smith growled, sweeping his arm back to administer another blow.

Holmes stepped forward.

"Desist, Smith!" he commanded. "And thou," Holmes thundered, turning angrily on the gathering, "Canst thou not see that ye frighten the wretch? Get thee away, in the name of mercy!"

Holmes turned to Smith as the settlers dispersed.

"This heathen be a man with a soul," he insisted. "It is not meet that he should be held in perpetual bondage."

"Call ye this the face of a *man*?" Smith demanded.

Holmes examined the stranger's features anew. *The blackamoor's countenance be exceeding peculiar,* he thought. *Be they men?* Lascivious curiosity surged within him. *I would fain examine the heathen. Yea, wouldst that I could be alone with him awhile,* he wished. Holmes admonished himself. *Shame! Thou art a man of God!*

"If a man this blackamoor be," Holmes declared, "he must receive the word of the Lord."

"These black dogs be made Christian?" cried Smith. "What, shall they be like us?"

Holmes's eyes lingered over the stranger. *Could they really be as we are?* he wondered.

Holmes hesitated, knowing well the dangerous yearning that lurked in his obsession with the stranger. The newcomer, he knew, had sparked into flame an old, boyish mischief—a sinful desire-- he thought long left behind.

"Doth he have a name?" Holmes asked.

"Aye, 'tis Pompey."

"Can he speak?"

Smith shook his head. "He can but squeal and gibber," he replied.

Holmes considered.

"I will examine the fellow," he said at length. "Bring him to me this afternoon."

Smith started to protest. Holmes adopted an officious tone.

"I will examine the lad to discern whether within him dwells a soul. Bathe him--" he instructed.

"*Bathe* him?" Smith cried. "Doth thou jest?"

"Bathe him and deliver him unto me in the Meeting House at four o' the clock this afternoon."

Holmes withdrew, burning with shame, for he knew that he was recklessly courting wickedness.

A fire crackled in the hearth of Obadiah Holmes's room that afternoon, as the preacher sat, grappling with his disturbing impulses. A wooden cross was the sole adornment on the whitewashed walls of the tiny room.

Thoughts stormed in Holmes's mind. He affected scholarly detachment to suppress his unseemly excitement. *Could the heathens be as we are?* he wondered. *I hath seen them working on the docks back in England. Aye, but never so close. Their skins be black as pitch! Their faces bear the aspect of gargoyles! Could the blood of Adam course through their veins, even as it doth in ours? It seems impossible to conceive. Be they men? Or be they of the ilk of witches and sprites?*

A vision of the stranger's rain-slickened body swam into Holmes's consciousness, forcing him to once again confront his shameful craving.

Holmes prayed for deliverance from the temptation that sorely troubled him, somewhat restoring his resolve. He turned his Bible to the Book of Isaiah to read again the verses about Ethiopians. A passage immediately leapt from the page.

In chains they shall come over, and they shall fall down unto thee; they shall make supplication unto thee, saying, "Surely God is in thee, and there is none else."

Holmes pondered the words. *Is that Thy design, O Lord, in bringing the stranger to us? The heathen arrived among us in chains-- and it is among us that he should acknowledge the Lord our God as his own? Do I divine Thy purpose, O Lord?*

A rap at the door interrupted Holmes's meditations. Smith's man entered, conveying the young captive in chains. The youth had been scrubbed clean and dressed in a white cotton nightshirt. He was panting in terror; his eyes fixed on Holmes.

Holmes was electrified by the dark stranger's presence. The sight of him garbed in a white nightdress was most appealing. *English dress doth temper thy savage aspect,* he mused.

"Unchain him," Holmes commanded the attendant. "And wait outside the door."

The manservant removed the stranger's restraints and withdrew. Holmes bolted the door behind him and regarded his trembling visitor.

"Canst thou speak English?" he asked.

The youth stared wide-eyed at Holmes, quaking. If he did understand, he was too frightened to answer.

"They call thee Pompey, do they not?"

A flicker of recognition stole across the young man's face, but he did not respond. The preacher daubed a piece of bread with lard and offered it to the stranger. The youth devoured it while Holmes lit candles.

In the dim light, the stranger's skin to Holmes seemed even darker. *On a moonless night,* he thought, *thou wouldst vanish utterly except for thine eyes!* He shivered slightly at the thought.

Holmes drew his visitor closer. The young man flinched and shied away.

"I will attend to thy wounds," Holmes soothed.

Holmes gingerly pivoted the youth to face away from him and untied the nightdress. Raw welts covered the stranger's back from the shoulder blades to the base of the spine.

"I pity thee, poor creature," the preacher commiserated, for his own back bore heavy scars from a whipping for heresy. "I, too, hath felt the cat o' nine tails."

Holmes gently applied salve to the young man's wounds and carefully replaced the nightshirt over his back. He guided his visitor nearer to the hearth, where the light was better. The youth was slender and shorter than he. Holmes judged him to be no more than twenty-one or twenty-two years old.

This blackamoor be undeniably fine of form, he reflected. *Mayhap not lesser than an English man. But his face! Such a coarse countenance surely marks dull wits.*

Holmes touched his hand to the youth's forearm and examined his fingers. *Thy skin's hue doth not besmirch mine own,* he observed. The young man flinched as Holmes put his nose to his arm and breathed of its scent. His skin smelled of lye soap.

Holmes examined the youth's arm by candlelight. The stranger's skin, he noted, was of a uniform brown color, and it appeared to be exceptionally smooth, almost hairless. Holmes observed that despite the skin's dark coloration, it glowed with a lustrous sheen from the firelight.

The smoothness of the skin was such that the contour of every muscle, every tendon and vein of the arm seemed visible in relief. It seemed to Holmes as if the youth's skin had been stretched tightly over his musculature.

Thrilled by his explorations, Holmes slid his grasp along the young man's forearm. Its silkiness was remarkable, though it was not so hairless as he had first perceived.

The preacher's hand reached the stranger's, and he grasped it into a fist. The skin of the hand was surprisingly rough so for one so young.

"Thou hast known toil," Holmes murmured.

Holmes extended the stranger's fingers and held them to the light. The bones of the digits seemed more prominent than his own, and the fingernails were long. The hands' dark, leathery integument and talon-like nails conjured in Holmes's mind a fleeting image of something birdlike and sinister. He shivered again.

Holmes turned the youth's palms upward, revealing a startling contrast of color. The palms were, he considered, of a more wholesome, if still impure color. Unlike the hands' brutish outer surface, the palms seemed to him graceful and expressive. *Be these the hands of a weaver… or perchance a musician?* he speculated.

Holmes glimpsed the young man's hair silhouetted in the candlelight and brought a candle closer to investigate. The hairs were a dense, wiry black tangle. He touched it. It seemed to him very odd, more like the wool of a sheep than the hair of a man, and like sheep's wool, its wiry texture could be compressed. *'T'must itch like a woolen nightcap,* Holmes thought. The young man winced as Holmes plucked a hair. He examined the black curl on his fingertip by the light of the candle. It appeared to be like a tiny coil. Holmes smiled. *How queer these creatures are!* he marveled.

Holmes caught himself. *Shame! Deceive not thyself. This way lies sin! Restrain this unseemly curiosity. Thou knowest that wantonness beckons. Heed not its call.*

Stifling his enthusiasm with scholarly affectation once more, Holmes turned his attention to his visitor's face. The young man cried out in apprehension as Holmes cupped his chin in his hands.

"Fear thee not," Holmes reassured him.

The youth continued to whimper, his eyes darting around the

room. Holmes put a finger to the stranger's lips to quieten him.

"Hush. I will not harm thee," he soothed.

The young man's breathing eased as his struggles subsided and the preacher resumed his inspection. The stranger had little beard, save for a scattering of curly whiskers that sprang from his chin. His cheekbones were high and his brows heavy. The ears were small. The lower lip was curiously pink, as was, from what Holmes could glimpse of it, the tongue. The teeth were quite white, though encrusted between them with yellow. *Thy countenance,* Holmes considered, revising his earlier judgment, *—save for the slack lips and broad nose—be not disagreeable… pleasing, even, after its own fashion.*

Looking into the stranger's eyes, Holmes was surprised to discover that his irises were not black at all, but of a deep brown color, quite distinct from the pupils. So absorbed was the preacher in his examination of his visitor that he only now realized that the young man was scrutinizing his own features. The youth's eyes searched Holmes's face, then met his gaze. In that instant, Obadiah Holmes was certain that he saw in those eyes not just intelligence, but a soul. A human soul.

Holmes's heart raced, so elated was he by his discovery, and thrilled by the stranger's exotic presence. He gently inclined the youth's head toward the candlelight to continue his investigation. As he did, he caught scent of a soapy, musky aroma wafting up from the nightshirt. He closed his eyes to savor the scent. *Verily,* he thought, *everything about this blackamoor doth quicken the blood.* Holmes chastised himself. *Wickedness! What queer passion hath this heathen unleashed? Old ghosts, trouble me not! Thou hast shared the marriage bed!* he told himself. *Thou hast sired many children! I must steel myself. Cavort not with the devil!*

Holmes stepped back, his mind a maelstrom of emotions. He gulped from a jug of water to compose himself. The stranger, sensing Holmes's agitation, stared at him anxiously.

Doth this be madness? Holmes wondered. *I must overbear this passion. I must withstand.* Yet even as he sought to calm the whirlwind in his mind, Holmes knew that he was all but powerless to stop.

The stranger's stance stiffened as Holmes drew him closer and began to delicately explore his physique with trembling hands. The youth flinched at his touch. Holmes's grasp glided over the outline of his form. The shoulders were bony and well-muscled, Holmes observed. The biceps were firm.

The beauty of the African is surely the most perfect of all races, he reflected. *Their silkiness of skin, leanness of form, and exotic guise all combine to beguile the eye! ...My blood runs hot. I must stop, ere I shall lose all reason.*

Holmes's eyes continued to survey the youth's physique, following the drape of the nightshirt over his collarbones and frame to the slight bulge between his legs. His glance darted uneasily toward the stranger's eyes, gleaming in the candlelight. An anxious consciousness met his gaze.

Holmes abruptly turned the young man away.

"Look not upon me," he snapped.

The youth began to whimper in fear.

Standing close behind the stranger now, Holmes glimpsed, down the neck of his shift, tightly coiled hairs dotting the brown skin of his chest. The spicy, musky odor of the young man's body again reached his nostrils, and he inhaled its scent. Desire flooded Holmes's being. The yearning felt as if it would consume his soul. *I am resistless,* he thought. *My wits have fled!*

Holmes slid his arm around the stranger's waist and grasped him tight. The youth cried out and tried to break free.

"*Daabi!* No!" he cried.

Holmes pressed his body against the stranger's. The youth's struggles increased, but Holmes held him fast, his free hand exploring his chest through the nightshirt.

"I will possess thee!" he murmured.

As the youth writhed and howled, Holmes's face pressed now against soft-prickly hair, now against silky skin. He drank in the stranger's bewitching scent. The warmth of the young man's body, his ebony skin, his delicious, tantalizing scent—*his forbiddenness*—thrilled Holmes more intensely than any sensation he had known before.

An urgent rapping on the door broke the spell. Startled, Holmes relaxed his grip. The terrified young man scrambled across the room.

"Hast thou come to harm, sir?" Smith's manservant demanded.

"N-nay," Holmes replied through the door. "Nay, all is well."

Holmes staggered back to the table. He gulped deeply from the jug, slowly recovering his senses. He looked at the panicked stranger, cowering on his haunches by the door. The youth's nightshirt had pulled up, and in the shadow of the garment, Holmes glimpsed his dark, dangling genitals. He closed his eyes tightly against the sight.

A sudden swell of revulsion and rage rose in Obadiah Holmes's breast. *Monstrous! Obscene!* Holmes beat his fists against his head, tears of shame burning in his eyes.

Holmes's fevered mind searched for an explanation. *How? How hath I been so deceived, that I am led astray? Thou knewest that this would lead unto sin, yet thou didst persist. How hath I been tempted so, Lord?* He pondered. *Devilry! Aye, 'tis the only answer. 'Tis him. 'Tis the creature.*

"Thou!" Holmes cried, pointing a trembling finger at the stranger. "Thou hast bewitched me!"

Yea, verily, Holmes thought. *Witchery, that was it. This satyr, this loathsome ram hath bewitched me, tempting me with his bestial carnality. Wickedness! 'Twas not the spark of humanity I saw in those eyes, but the very flames of Hellfire! Oh, how artful is thy trickery, Satan!*

Holmes fell to his knees, weeping as he prayed.

"Have mercy upon me, O Lord," he begged. "Forgive me for my sins. I heeded not the danger. I have been foolish and wicked," he sobbed.

Holmes wiped away his tears and gazed again at the frightened stranger crouching in the shadows. The sight recalled to his mind a story from the Scriptures, the story of Ham from Genesis.

Ham saw the nakedness of his father, Noah, and God brought upon Ham's progeny a curse for all time.

Then another thought occurred to Holmes, one that filled him with dread. *Hath I not seen the stranger's nakedness, just as Ham saw Noah's? Am I, too, to be cursed?* He began to weep again.

"Have pity upon me, Lord," he prayed. "I knew not. I knew not!"

As his tears subsided, a new understanding dawned. *Say not the scholarly books that Cush-- in Africa-- was the land of Ham's seed? Yea, verily. Africans be the accursed sons of Ham! Their blackness a spectacle of disobedience to all the world! These creatures be not of mankind: one could no more baptize one of these things than one could a bullock. How witless of me to have conceived such a thing.*

Holmes wiped away his tears. Thoughts continued to unfold, one upon the last.

If these demons hath power to tempt even me, what of a feeble-headed woman? What sorcery could they practice upon them? The thought of those vile hands rending the flesh of our womenfolk-- English womenfolk! Defiling their purity with their intemperate lusts... 'twas unspeakable!

Holmes resumed his prayer.

"O Lord," he pleaded, "deliver us from evil. I see now Thy purpose in revealing to me the heathens' wicked natures. Thou hath sent these accursed sons of Ham to be our servants in this land of Thy blessing. We shall be watchful, guarding against their wickedness. They will be kept in due obedience, lest they cast off the yoke and bring ruin upon us all. I shall be Thine instrument, O Lord. Thy will be done. Amen."

Obadiah Holmes stood up and composed his robes, gazing contemptuously at the stranger.

"Thou art black with God's curse, foul heathen," he sneered. "Thou art damned for all eternity."

Holmes unbolted the door and called the attendant.

"Return this creature to thine master," he instructed the man. "He canst do with him what he will."

The Testament of Okyerema Mireku

1826

The elders of the Newport Colored Union Church gathered in Isaac Rice's modest home after worship, as they did each Sunday afternoon. The curtains of the front room stirred on a welcome breeze on the muggy June day. As Violet Rice served lemonade, Isaac placed a muslin-wrapped packet tied with a ribbon on the table before Shadrack Hawkins and his wife, Betsey.

"Such a fat parcel!" Betsey exclaimed. "How could you resist opening it? I surely couldn't have waited."

"Don't you think that Newport would have wanted us to read his news together, Sister Hawkins?" Isaac replied.

Isaac put on his wire-rimmed spectacles, untied the ribbon, and unfolded the cloth. As he removed a sheaf of papers tied with twine, a small envelope slipped from between the sheets.

"There seems to be a letter, too," Isaac said. "Which shall I read first?"

"The big one," Betsey said. "They always say 'long letters carry good news'."

"Yes," agreed Violet.

Issac untied the twine and scanned the document.

"It's a testament," he said. "*The Testament of Okyerema Mireku.*"

"That ridiculous name he uses," Betsey scoffed.

"It's his African name," Shadrack reminded her.

"The name he was born with," agreed Isaac.

"I still say it's ridiculous," insisted Betsey. "Everybody knows him as Newport Gardner."

"They don't know him at all where he's gone," Shadrack said. "Maybe he thinks it will put the Africans at their ease."

"Imagine going all that way at his age," Violet sighed. "I still can't get over it."

"He's wanted to return all his life," Shadrack said.

"Come on," Betsey said, "Let's hear the news. Read it."

"His handwriting is as beautiful as ever," Isaac observed. "Though it is a little uneven. Maybe it was written at sea. It's dated January third."

Isaac began to read aloud.

I, Okyerema Mireku, with joy in my heart, record this testament to the truth of the Gospel. For I believe that my story is a lesson that faith in God and repentance of sins is the sure path to salvation.

I was born eight decades ago, in a land of green luxuriance; a place that they call the Gold Coast. My family were griots *by profession, troubadours who roamed the land, telling tales in word and song. Under my uncle's tutelage, I learned to play the horn and the* dondo *drum, and my mother taught me many songs and poems. My uncle also taught me to carve the Adinkra symbols for the moral of each fable, charms which we would barter for food.*

I was fourteen years old when I last saw my mother's face. We were, all of us, captured by the raiding party of a hostile chief and brought to a fort on the coast. I was separated there from my mother and uncle and know not of their fate. Seeing my mother behind bars of iron, I knew that I would never hear her sweet voice again.

I was purchased by a Newport sea captain almost immediately. The sea crossing held many horrors, though it was not as bad for me as for some. I sang to keep my fears at bay, and because of this, I was made one of the captain's privilege slaves. This meant that I had the freedom of the deck, serving food, and amusing the crew with my singing. Whenever I could, I stole down below to tend the wounds and sores of my unlucky fellows in the hold.

After a six-week voyage, we reached the island of St. Kitts, where most of the wretched Africans were disembarked and sold. At length we arrived in Newport. Oh, how my heart ached for my mother, my family, and the land of my birth! Alone at nights, I cried anguished tears until I could shed no more. But by day, I learned to put on the servile mask of a slave that was now mine to wear.

The Newport sea captains at this time vied to outdo one another in the opulence of their homes, their gardens, or in Captain Caleb Gardner's case, his music room. I suppose I was a curiosity to a lover of music, an African boy who sang many strange airs, so Captain Gardner purchased me, and became my master. It was he who gave me the name Newport Gardner.

My master and his wife took a great interest in my songs, unfamiliar as they were to their ears. Mrs. Gardner enrolled me in the school of Mr. Law, a very fine teacher of music. There I learned to play the piano and violin and the rudiments of composition, and I improved my command of the English language. This was aided by my master's permission to borrow books from his library. In the evenings, I read and practiced my penmanship, remembering how I had traced the Adinkra symbols years before. As I grew into adulthood, my duties gradually became more in the nature of a secretary to the captain and tutor to his children.

I was mindful of the Gardners' kindness and the privileges that I enjoyed, though the abuse that I received when I stepped outside the home reminded me that I was a pariah in my new land. Even so, my treatment was as nothing to that dealt to most Africans. When we journeyed once to Portsmouth, I saw the slaves on the farms there, Akan, Fulani, and people from unfamiliar regions. I witnessed them laboring almost as beasts of burden, their faces haggard and hollow, their bodies grown old before their time. I am haunted to this day by their specters.

Betsey sucked her teeth in disapproval.

"Shame," she murmured.

"Things are little better for them now that they are free," Shadrack lamented.

Isaac resumed reading.

It was around this time that love for Christ was enkindled in my soul. For the first time in many years, I knew joy, joy at admitting the Lord into my heart. A flame was sparked which burns in me still, though I confess that I was, at first, plagued by doubt.

For even as my Christian faith deepened, I struggled to understand how a righteous God could permit the calamitous state of the people on the farms that I had seen, and the yet more wretched condition of the plantation slaves in the southern territories and the West Indies. I grieved for the unhappy state of the Africans in my native land, mired as they were in heathenish darkness, foolish and wicked enough to sell one another into slavery. How could these immense evils, I wondered, be God's plan?

"How indeed?" Isaac commented. He continued reading.

I spent many hours in reflection and prayer searching for an answer. The African, I came to understand, not having received the word of the Lord, is in a state of nature; he is idolatrous, worshipping trees, and streams, and reptiles. He serves divers lusts and pleasures which lead to dissipation and wickedness, and earns him, living among Christian people, the deserved reproach of his neighbors. Only when the sons of Africa are called and converted, and made sensible of their unregenerate state, can they stretch out their hands to God, and feel sorrow for their sins.

When I read the words of Jeremiah, I suddenly saw the design of the Almighty in bringing us to America. The revelation inspired me, at the age of eighteen, to compose an anthem:

The days come, saith the Lord, that I will cause my people of Israel and Judah to return to the land that I gave to their fathers, and they shall possess it. Therefore, fear thou not, O my servant Jacob, I will save thee from afar, and thy seed from their captivity, and Jacob shall return and be in rest and quiet, and none shall make him afraid. Amen. Hear the words of the Lord, O ye African race, hear the words of promise! Praise ye the Lord. Trust in the Lord, O African! Hallelujah. Amen.

Reverend Samuel Hopkins of the Congregational Church was delighted with my Promise *anthem and invited me to sing it at services. Dr. Hopkins was an abolitionist and friend of the negro, and I became a frequent visitor to his fireside. I was deeply touched by the sincerity of his sympathy for the benighted Africans. I adopted with enthusiasm his idea that freed slaves should return to Africa and spread the word of the Lord. I prayed ever harder for my freedom so that I might become a missionary and work for Africa's salvation.*

It was not unknown for slaves in Newport to be permitted to work for their own profit in whatever time could be gained for extra diligence in their duties. Thanks to my master's indulgence, I was able to compose melodies in this "gained" time and to perform them at recitals. The modest notoriety that this earned me led many people to seek instruction in the art of singing. Soon I rented a room above a shop on Thames Street and spent all of my gained hours as a singing-school master. I began to save money.

Around this time, I received the greatest blessing of my life. An Akan elder in the town introduced me to a girl of my clan who was a maid in the Wanton house. Limas was beautiful and strong-willed and pious, and after a brief courtship, we obtained the consent of our masters to wed. Limas was my devoted and beloved helpmate for thirty-five years, and she bore me six daughters and four sons. She also kept alive my Akan tongue.

"What a beautiful soul Limas was," sighed Violet.

"They were perfectly matched," agreed Betsey.

Isaac resumed reading.

My singing school, which was numerously attended, thrived, but I was still far from saving enough money to purchase my freedom and that of my wife. My duties for Captain Gardner-- bookkeeping, correspondence, et cetera-- were by now, almost effortless for me, and so valuable an assistant to him had I become, that he permitted me move out of his home and rent a house of my own where I might raise my family. Pope Street, or Negro Lane as it is known, was where other Africans who had prospered (relative to their fellows) had settled. Among them were Prince Almy, Zingo Stevens, and Caesar Lyndon. These men were, like me, slaves, though slaves employed in occupations requiring literacy and numeracy or in one of the skilled trades.

Then came upon us revolution and war, and three years of occupation by British troops. Trade came to a standstill. Many a Newport merchant was ruined by the war. Others fled. We slaves stayed or went according to our masters' whims. Fortunately, Captain Gardner and Mr. Wanton, who owned Limas, decided to remain, so we were not parted. Other husbands and wives, mothers and children, were separated at this time, to their immense grief. So many people left the town that abandoned houses were torn down for firewood. I clung on by my fingernails, depleting most of the money I had saved for the family's freedom.

When the war ended, the men of wealth hoped that prosperity might return on its former basis, but a hostile England meant that the islands of the West Indies were closed to Newport's vessels. The town's days of splendor were at an end. The depression of business meant that things grew even worse for the Africans. Many of the farm slaves were freed, only to become penniless vagrants. Those fortunate men in the African community, like me, felt a sense of responsibility toward our brothers and sisters, and we resolved to form a benevolent society to try to lift up our fellow Africans.

Our African Union Society was to be supported by the subscriptions of its members, with the object of providing for burials, the support of widows, and for the education of our children. We hoped to establish a fund for loans to enable Africans to purchase land or build homes. In other words, we aimed to improve the material and spiritual welfare of the Africans, and hoped that, with the sympathy and goodwill of the men around us, we would one day be admitted to the ranks of citizens. I have always believed that every pious man is a good citizen of the whole world.

Two remarkable events occurred in my forty-sixth year, anno Domini 1791. Some will think my account savors of a tall story, but it is true, and I regard it as nothing more than an evident, if extraordinary answer to prayer. It was my habit as a young man to make the occasional wager, and on this occasion, I and four other slaves bought a ticket in the Massachusetts semi-annual lottery. It drew a prize of two thousand dollars. This boon, of which my share was four hundred dollars, was a cause for great celebration. But it was not money enough to purchase my liberty and also that of my wife and children.

Certain that this shortfall was a sign from God, I decided to spend my gained time in fasting and prayer. I told no one but Limas of my plan and spent my next gained day in solitary prayer for my liberation and that of my family. My master, ignorant of my occupation, sent for me late in the afternoon. He was told that it was my gained day but insisted that I should attend him. When at length I called upon him, the captain handed me a piece of paper, on which was written:

I, Caleb Gardner, of Newport, Rhode Island, do this day manumit and release forever Newport Gardner, his wife, and children.

I fell to my knees and clasped the captain's hand in mine, weeping with joy and gratitude. Still more gratitude did I feel to Almighty God for freeing me before I had even finished my supplication! Was there ever such a sign of His love for our people, and of His desire that we should place our faith in Him?

I resolved that that I should work for the rest of my life for the good of souls. I left the captain's service, forever in his debt, and became sexton at the First Congregational Church. I and others of the African Union Society continued our feeble efforts to help our fellow men as more and more became free. But our people were being shunned. With conditions as they were, few could find work, and many were forced to live in shacks and huts on the edge of the town.

Alas, though we of the Union Society did our best to nurture the colored people of Newport, we were hindered by the backwardness and impoverishment of the very people whom we sought to help. Discouragement, listlessness, and hunger extinguished people's hope. They descended into drunkenness, covetousness, and squabbling. Children were neglected. I started a free school for boys and girls but could not sustain it. Exhortations to attend church fell on deaf ears because the people resented being made to sit up in pigeonholes out of sight.

Seeking to improve the morals of our people, Shadrack Hawkins, Isaac Rice, I, and others met and agreed to form a Christian church of our own and to hold communion together. We obtained funds from the various churches that the people attended, discovering them as eager to be rid of us Africans as we were to worship together. To my immense gratification, the Colored Union Church opened its doors to its first communicants two years ago. I pray that it will survive and flourish.

The attitude of the churchmen did not surprise me, for I had some years before been wounded by the words of Dr. Hopkins, who had so influenced me in my youth. I thought that Dr. Hopkins's encouragement of emigration to Africa to spread the Gospel arose purely from righteousness and benevolence. As he began to speak publicly, however, I came to understand that this pious man, whom I loved, considered the presence of free men of color in America to be a great injury to the white inhabitants and that our removal would deliver them from a great calamity!

The scales fell from my eyes upon hearing these words. So true it is that faithful are the wounds of a friend; for Dr. Hopkins was speaking the truth as he saw it. I knew from that moment that we Africans were forever to be strangers and outcasts in a strange land, attended by many disadvantages and evils, for as long as we and our descendants remained in the country. I had a sudden revelation that my mission must be not just to return to Africa to spread the word of the Lord, but to entreat the Africans in America to follow me.

I cannot now conceive how I once believed in a bright future for our people. In our innocence we did not understand that white men cannot for a moment see past our skins. We thought of ourselves as Africans, just as the Englishmen thought of themselves. But they see not people with souls, but our skins only. Our very flesh marks us out to them as inferior, impure. Objects of spite.

So many white men—friendly white men—have told me that it is the unfamiliarity of our faces that so unnerves them. That they are unaccustomed to seeing us among them. I wanted to shout out, go to God's Little Acre and see the resting places of our grandfathers! How long will it take for our faces to become familiar to you?

Now they have disenfranchised us. The right to vote that I exercised as a free man for three score years has been withdrawn. They say that we lack the education or intelligence to act responsibly. The same people who bar us from the schools!

I feel sure that there is something more at the bottom of all this. If I did not know the white men better, I would say it was shame; I think that fear might better describe it. Fear that has seeped into their bones. Knowing well the sins that they have committed against us, the white men dare not face their consciences. Our presence is an everlasting reminder to them of the judgment of the all-wise that awaits them, and they despise us for it. The malignancy grows with each generation. Reason is driven out by fear; hatred extinguishes Christian charity. I fear where will it end for our people.

They say that the strong do what they will and the weak suffer what they must: so it has been for the African. But, dear friends, we free Africans have a choice. I return to Africa to set an example for my fellows. Verily it is an enterprise fraught with danger, with violent storms, disease, and warring clans awaiting us. But if die we must to take up the Lord's work and liberate the Africans in America, I face that prospect gladly. Christ died to make men holy: we will die to make them free.

Hear the words of the Lord, O ye African race, hear the words of promise! Like Jacob, we can return to the land of our fathers and possess it. All we must do is repent our sins, praise God, and do His work. Trust in the Lord, my brothers!

How my heart sings as I near home. Newport Gardner of old is no more. Hallelujah! Okyerema Mireku returns with joy in his heart, and the word of the Lord on his lips. Hallelujah! Amen. Okyerema Mireku, Dated this 3rd of January, A. D. 1826

"Hallelujah, indeed," Violet said. "He is finally saving souls in Africa! Just think of it."

"He writes strong words about white men's hatred for us," said Shadrack, "but they are true."

"He could never speak so plainly here," agreed Isaac. "He no longer has to hold his tongue. He can finally speak his mind."

"Do you think that people will follow him to Africa?" asked Betsey.

Isaac looked doubtful.

"With all the dangers that he writes about, I think people will be scared to," he replied. "Besides, Newport—" he corrected himself, "*Okyerema* is an old man, and he doesn't understand that the people no longer think of themselves as Africans. They are *negroes* now, not quite at home in America yet, but no longer African, either."

"Somewhere in between," agreed Shadrack.

"Read the other letter," urged Betsey, "Let's see what it says."

Isaac opened the envelope and unfolded the letter. He read aloud.

Monrovia, April 18th, 1826. My dear Rice, It is with great sorrow that I inform you of the fate of your friends--

Isaac gasped. He re-read the passage.

It is with great sorrow that I inform you of the fate of your friends, late of the town of Newport, who took their leave of you December last.

Following a service of consecration for the infant church for the colony of Cape Mesurado and the unanimous acclaim of Mr. Newport Gardner and Mr. John Salmar Nubia as deacons, our party sailed from Boston on the morning of 4th January inst. After a pleasant passage of about five weeks, we arrived at the colony at Monrovia, little suspecting the fate that awaited us.

Isaac's voice began to quaver.

After being there for ten days, a number of our party succumbed to the fever of these climes. It grieves me almost beyond expression to inform you that Deacon Gardner, Deacon Nubia, Ahama Gardner, and my own wife and son were all fatally afflicted. One quarter of our number perished within six weeks of our arrival here.

Tears streamed down Isaac Rice's face as he read on.

Deacon Gardner was joyful until the end, having truly placed his life in the hands of God. I close with the words of his farewell message, which I recorded as he spoke them on the eve of our departure. "I go to set an example to the youth of my race. I go to encourage the young. They can never be elevated here. I have tried it sixty years-- it is in vain. Could I, by my example, lead them to set sail, and I die the next day, I should be satisfied." Yours sincerely, I remain, sir, Your servant, John Chevers

Reminiscences

2025

Yellow leaves fluttered down from the trees above Michael Chiappetta's head as he sat by the bike path on a glorious late November day. Puffs of white streaked across the sapphire sky. A chilly breeze heralded the imminence of winter, but the sun's warmth was still pleasant on Michael's bald head.

An SUV crunched to a halt in the gravel at the roadside. Peter Chiappetta bounded from the vehicle. The car chirped electronically as he locked it.

"Hey!" Peter cried, embracing his younger brother heartily. Peter Chiappetta was a heavy, enthusiastic man of sixty-five, energetic and animated despite his bulk.

"Happy Thanksgiving," he said.

"Happy belated Thanksgiving to you," replied Michael.

"Hey, thanks for coming down," Peter said. "I know it's a long way for you."

"It was a great idea. I haven't been to this place since a school field trip. Besides, it's only an hour and a half," Michael said. "What is it they say about Rhode Islanders? If you're going to drive more than forty-five minutes, you pack a lunch. How's Ellen?"

"Fine. She's shopping with Susan."

"How was yesterday?"

"It was great, just Ellen and me and Susan and the kids. You?"

"I went to Caitlyn and A.J.'s for dinner. Dylan is four, if you can believe it."

"Jeez," Peter said, shaking his head, "He was just a baby last time I saw him. Are you heading back to Boston tonight?"

"Yeah. I've got a pile of essays to mark this weekend. I'm not a retiree, you know," Michael teased.

"You ain't that far behind," Peter responded, joining his brother on the bench. "Hey, do you mind if we sit here for a minute? I've got some stuff to show you."

Michael zipped up his jacket.

"Sure," he said. "It's a little breezy, but I was enjoying the sunshine."

"You know that genealogical research that I've been doing online? I've found some amazing stuff," Peter said, pulling a manila envelope from his windbreaker, and taking out some papers. "I did this family tree. Isn't it amazing what you can find online now? I managed to trace a Chiappetta ancestor back to the 1830s."

"Wow! That is amazing. Have you managed to track down our tiny-bottomed ancestor?"

Peter frowned.

"Chiappetta is a proud name," he said.

Michael laughed.

"It's a diminutive term for buttocks."

"I'm proud of my Calabrese ancestry."

"I am, too. I just think it's a mystery how we got that name."

"Doesn't matter. Anyway, the earliest ancestor I found is a Giacomo Chiappetta, baptized in 1834 in San Nicola, down near the tip of the boot. He married Elena, no maiden name recorded, in 1852. And look at this! She had twelve children. Can you imagine? She was pregnant pretty much non-stop from the age of seventeen until she died sometime in her forties. She was our... let's see... great... great... grandmother."

"Wow."

"Our great-grandfather, her son, Vicente—he was one of the later children--came to America in, uh, 1896. Two years later, he met Filomena Berardi, our great-grandmother," Peter said, taking some photos from the envelope and filing through them. "And here…" he said, "here is Filomena."

"Beautiful."

"She was what they called a Gibson Girl. The swept-up hairstyle, the high collar, and the cameo pin?"

"I thought *I* was the history professor. Bet she did her spine in wearing that corset."

"Probably," Peter chuckled. He pointed to a photograph as he handed them to Michael. "And this one is the meat market Vicente worked in up on Federal Hill. Look how it was all decorated for Fourth of July."

"Looks to be the early 1900s. People were really patriotic then."

"They were grateful to the country that gave them such a good life. Back in Calabria, they were poor," Peter said, shaking his head. "Poor like you can't imagine. They came here, worked hard, they built businesses, bought houses… it was like a miracle for them. And the whole family living in one tenement house: *nonno* and *nonni* on the first floor, mom and pop upstairs, and auntie and uncle on the third floor. They loved this country because they found freedom and such good fortune here."

"Hmm," agreed Michael, looking through the photos.

"It always amazes me how beautifully they're dressed in photographs," said Peter. "All the men in suit and tie and hat in the middle of summer! And the women in their white summer dresses, always brilliant white."

"How can you tell from a black and white photo?"

"That's true. I hadn't thought of that. But they must have been white-- they always look so dazzling. And it makes me think, these were poor people -- I mean, a lot better off than when they were in the old country -- but still poor. Practically everyone was poor back then. I mean, how did they afford the clothes?"

"There were tailors in every neighborhood, or they made their own," Michael replied. "*Nonni* made all her own clothes, even some of ours, as kids, if you remember."

"And think of all the work for the women," Peter marveled. "Washing clothes by hand with yellow soap—hanging them out to dry, ironing— and those old irons had to be heated on the coal stove."

"…Cooking, baking, housecleaning, and all for huge families," added Michael. "It's no wonder Filomena looks worn out in this one." He flipped through the photos. "Who's in this one? I recognize the young man, that's dad, but is that *Nonno*?"

"That's *Nonno*."

"My God," exclaimed Michael. "He was so young."

"And the old, old man with the wonderful mustache is Vicente. And do you know who this is, the infant on Vicente's knee?"

"You, I'm guessing?"

Peter smiled.

"Me."

"You were so cute!" Michael laughed. He eyed his brother, adding, "Now look at you."

"I have no recollection of him," Peter said. "I must have been around two years old when he died. But it's incredible when you think about it. Four generations in one photo."

"And a living link to Italy, too," Michael added. "Our great-grandfather, who was born… when?"

"Um, 1869."

"Our great-grandfather, born in Calabria way back in the 1860s; *Nonno*, the first generation born in the United States; and dad and you; the second and third generations."

"For me, that picture really brings home the closeness of our connection with Italy," Peter said.

"It really is close, when you see it like that, I mean, four generations in one photo."

Peter returned the photos to the envelope and put it in his pocket.

"I'll email the family tree to you," he said.

"Thanks. I'd really like that," Michael said, rising. "Are we gonna walk this bike path or what?"

The brothers ambled along the asphalt path as it traced a gentle curve through the woods. Not far off the road stood a dilapidated old house, its roof sagging. Though the structure looked uninhabitable, a curl of smoke rose from the chimney. The yard was littered with commercial fishing gear and rusting tools, blanketed by orangey pine needles. An ancient, lichen-encrusted stone wall bordered the property, intersecting with another old ruin of stone that stretched far into the woods. The men walked on.

A biker whizzed past. The trees flanking the pavement grew denser the farther the brothers got from the road. Scattered everywhere in the woods were large, gray granite boulders, come to rest where glaciers had shed them.

"This used to be a branch railroad line," Michael said.

"A streetcar line?" asked Peter.

"More or less. The trains ran to Narragansett Pier. Probably a real holiday mood in summer, open carriages and all that. Cars carrying men in shirt and tie and Panama hats—like we saw in the photos-- and women in summer dresses, with those enormous hats they wore. They came from near and far to swim or to stroll on the promenade by the shore for a day. The rich folks, I imagine, stayed in hotels and gambled the night away at the casino. But they all came down on this line. It was a very democratic means of transportation, the streetcar. I mean, the poor and the well-to-do traveling together."

"I remember *Nonno* used to talk about the streetcars in Providence. He loved trolleys. He could never understand why they got rid of 'em."

"Cars," replied Michael. "It was the tire manufacturers who wanted to boost car sales, so they bought up the streetcar companies, ripped out the lines and scrapped all the trolleys."

"Corporations are always the villain for you, aren't they?"

"I'm a labor historian, so I'm hardly a neutral."

The path approached a scrubby clearing off to the left where a cast-iron fence guarded a handful of graves. It was posted with a state historic cemetery marker. The brothers stopped to take a look. Peter gingerly picked through the undergrowth to investigate.

"The headstones are all covered with stuff," he said. He reached through the fence and picked away at some lichen on one of the gravestones. "Latham. 1803... 73 years... That's a ripe old age for that time."

"Must have been a farm here."

"You can see stone walls in the woods all along here."

"Hard to believe this could have been farmland once. Imagine trying to grow anything in this rocky soil."

"Maybe it was pasture."

"Maybe."

Peter brushed his hands off as he returned to the pavement. The men continued along.

The trees thinned as the surrounding woods gradually opened up to reveal an expansive swamp. The bike path's embankment traversed a watery, dead forest. Gray remnants of trees poked like desiccated fingers into the sky, their bony shapes elongated by reflections in the leaf-stained water. A few saplings perched on grassy tufts here and there, sustaining an existence amid the deluge. The brothers paused to take in the scene. Water trickled through a corrugated pipe beneath their feet, sunk for drainage. Eddies swirled from the pipe's outflow, carrying tiny yellow maple leaves which circled and lazily floated away.

"The Great Swamp," announced Peter.

"Yeah. Though the famous fight actually took place a little ways from here. In the 1600s, the English colonists and some of their Indian allies burned the Narragansett tribe's fort in the swamp and massacred hundreds of women and children. A lot of the Narragansett warriors managed to escape, and the following year they took their revenge, burning the English settlements all along the bay up to Providence."

Peter's eyes narrowed.

"You actually know all that?"

Michael chuckled.

"I looked it up," he admitted.

Peter grunted.

"The Narragansett reservation is just down the road in Charlestown," he said. "Though you'll find that most of the "Narragansetts" here today are Black."

"That's because the Indians were enslaved. They intermarried with Black slaves."

""*Narragansetts*,"" Peter snorted mockingly.

Michael paused, looking quizzically at his brother.

"Why do you and I always seem to talk about Black people these days?" he asked.

"I don't know. They're just so in-your-face at the moment. Every ad on TV has to have a Black face. This woke business is getting too much."

Something caught Michael's eye and he nudged his brother.

"An egret!" he whispered, pointing out a large bird perched motionless atop a towering splinter. All at once the bird extended its long wings and leapt from its perch, taking to the air with slow, graceful strokes. Its wingspan disappeared into the thicker woods at the swamp's edge. The brothers ambled along.

"It's all this protesting and complaining lately," said Peter. "The violence, the looting. How is looting two-hundred-dollar sneakers doing anything to advance their cause? It's doing the opposite."

"From what I've seen," responded Michael, "it's not only Black people committing violence. There are all sorts of troublemakers piling on to this."

"Yeah, well speaking of violence, did you see in the paper about those six men? The Providence police are calling it the worst crime they've ever investigated. Gang-raped a sixteen-year-old girl. Did you see their pictures? Six of them, all Black."

"Yeah, I saw that. Terrible. Absolutely disgusting. Though they looked more mixed race to me, maybe Hispanic."

"Whatever. But you ask me why people are afraid of Black men? You're damn right they're afraid of them. They have good reason to be."

The forest of maples and birches grew denser as the path left the swamp. A bower-like canopy of branches arched over the men's heads. Billowy white clouds raced against the blue of the sky through the tangled latticework. There was the distant rat-a-tat-tat of a woodpecker, then a sudden squeal of brakes from behind. Peter pulled Michael onto the grass border to let a pair of cyclists pass. Leaves rustled underfoot as the brothers briefly walked along the path's edge.

"So," Michael asked, "when you see a picture of a White man who's committed a terrible crime... a serial killer, say, do you think he's representative of the White race?"

"No."

"But when the face is black, you project that judgment onto an entire race of people?"

"I know the point you're trying to make, but that's not how it is," Peter objected. "Look, would you feel safe going out at night in Roxbury, or South Providence? Would you? God forbid you would go there -- but would you feel safe?"

"No..."

"Well, there you are. I'll tell you what the difference is between Black people and the Italians, the Irish, the Portuguese, everybody else. It's culture. Our ancestors had discipline," Peter said. "They had standards of behavior, a work ethic, and they were frugal."

"They stuck together as a community, and they helped each other," agreed Michael.

"Exactly. They had shared standards of behavior. Culture. It was a culture they brought with them, and it was a culture of survival. They went to church, they respected authority, and the kids had a strict upbringing. Look at us. Was anyone ever allowed to call us "Pete" or "Mike"? No, Ma would have killed any kid that tried to. First them and then us. It was always Peter and Michael."

"And your point is?" asked Michael.

"Black people don't have that discipline. They don't have a culture, or what they do have is a self-destructive one, and that's why they're stuck where they are."

"Are you serious? You're saying Black people don't have culture?"

"Not a constructive one. The crime? The women having baby after baby, all by different fathers… and where are the fathers?" Peter gave an exaggerated shrug. "Out screwing another woman! And she'll milk the system for benefits, too. And do you call all that bling and glamorizing violence and mistreating women that their rappers do culture? I sure don't."

Michael shook his head.

"I've got news for you," he said. "Way back when Vicente and Filomena were courting, at the turn of the twentieth century? The music they were dancing to was Black music. Virtually all American music —American popular music -- is Black music. And today, hip-hop is a cultural phenomenon in practically every country around the globe."

"Yeah? Well, maybe," Peter continued, "But that doesn't excuse the lack of responsibility that they take for their own problems."

"Problems like lack of access to a decent education? Is that their responsibility?"

"Give me a break. I was a high school principal for twenty years. Do they value education? Do the parents make sure their kids go to school, encourage them to achieve?"

"I agree that there's a value placed on education in some cultures in a way that's often lacking in the Black community," conceded Michael.

"Often? Almost always."

"But if the parents were failed by the schools, and their parents were, and so on going back, and if time and again you're denied opportunities even if you do work hard and try to achieve, and you're knocked back every time, that's a generational problem, almost a cultural inheritance."

Peter nodded in satisfaction.

"Thank you. That's what I mean about a destructive culture."

"But it sounds to me as if you're blaming people for disadvantages that they've been born into."

Peter stopped and turned to his brother.

"Your grandparents were born into disadvantage. Did that stop them?" he demanded. "They were poor. Do you think they had an education? Do you think that people back then welcomed Italians with open arms?"

"Times were different then. Plus, skin color is a different thing altogether. You can see a Black person from across the street, and already you're making judgments about who they are."

Peter moved on.

"You've got an answer for everything don't you?" he said. "I've said it before, and I'll say it again, P-H-D: Piled High and Deep."

Michael sighed.

"Unconscious bias is a well-documented phenomenon," he said. "The fact is that Black people's experience of life is different from ours, in hundreds of different ways, probably every day of their lives."

"Oh, here we go. "White privilege"."

"You can't deny that being White makes a difference to one's life chances."

"*Ma dai*!" Peter muttered under his breath.

"I think you'd see things differently if you walked a mile in a Black person's shoes," Michael said.

The path led through a dense area of evergreens. It felt considerably colder in the shade. A scent of pine wafted on a freshening breeze, sending bits from the trees pirouetting to the ground. A carpet of rust-colored needles covered either side of the path, from which a forest of trunks jutted, extending into the half-shadow.

Peter zipped his jacket.

"When I took early retirement," he said, "I volunteered for a program in the town to help disadvantaged kids, especially minorities, in schools. I volunteered for a year and a half. I offered my time, not just attending board meetings in the evenings, but also working one-to-one with kids —most of them Black -- after school. You know why I gave up? It wasn't the kids -- the kids were great. It was the parents. The school arranged parent/teacher evenings to meet the parents and discuss how their kids were doing. No one would turn up. You know what they had to do? Advertise that there'd be free food. They'd get a full house."

"If that's what worked, maybe they should've offered refreshments every time," Michael suggested.

Peter snorted.

"They can't be bothered to show when it's their kids' education, but they'll turn up for free sandwiches and potato chips? I don't get it. I just don't get it. And I can tell you I got nothing but hostility from the Black board members of that program. They'd just sit there and scowl at you. One board member accused me of racism. At a board meeting of an organization to help minority children that I was volunteering my time to, I was accused of being a racist!"

"I can understand how White people can sometimes be perceived as patronizing."

"Oh, for Christ's sake. There's real hostility and hatred. They don't want "whitey's" help, at least the ones I've come across don't."

Michael stopped. Water trickled in a shallow ditch by the roadway. Somewhere in the branches a blue jay screeched. He turned to Peter in puzzlement.

"Where's all this anger coming from?" he asked.

Peter shrugged.

"It's all this stuff in the news. The demands, the accusations of injustice. It's non-stop. They're on the streets shouting everywhere. You can't open your mouth these days without somebody accusing you of being racist."

"You know what?" Michael said. "I'm getting kinda cold. What do you say we head back to the cars?" His brother half-shrugged again, and the two men turned back.

"Our efforts to help in the town were shunned and rejected," Peter continued. "I tried but they don't want our help. They don't want help from any of us."

"Hang on, who is they?"

"Black people. Or, I should say, a certain class of Black people."

"I think you're making massive generalizations."

"You know what I can't understand?" asked Peter, "They complain so much about racism in this country, why don't they go to a country where they wouldn't face discrimination?"

"Are you serious? Send them back to Africa?" Michael asked. "Can you imagine what you'd say if someone suggested Italian Americans go back to Italy? You'd be outraged, and rightly so."

"That's not what I'm saying, and you know it. I'm just saying that if racism is so intolerable in this country, why don't they *voluntarily* go someplace where it won't be an issue for them?"

"That's… words fail me. That's just wrong on so many levels. You're saying that Black Americans should have to go to Africa to find a better life?"

"Of course I'm not saying that. What I'm saying is that it's high time that Black people took a little responsibility for their problems instead of blaming everybody else. Fix the problems in your own community, I say. Clean up the drugs, control your feral kids --close your legs while you're at it -- and get a job maybe," Peter stormed. "Instead of whining about other people, pull up your own bootstraps."

"It helps if you've got bootstraps to start with," rejoined Michael.

A jogger huffed past as the men reached the embankment across the swamp. Under cloud, and with the light starting to fade, the scene looked bleaker than before. Barren spikes of trees pierced a yellowish sky; the still brown waters and scrubby islets seemed devoid of all life.

"You have just totally swallowed all that woke crap, haven't you?" Peter said, with a hollow chuckle. "Every other group of people in this country has bettered themselves over time. The Irish were on the bottom rung at first, but they worked their way into the police and local politics and wound up taking them over. The Italians were next, dirt poor at first, but with a lot of hard work, they set up small businesses, got ahead. The Jews? Same thing, on steroids. Now it's the Hispanics. They've only been here, what, thirty, forty years? Now they own houses in the city and rent them to the Blacks! Every other group of people progresses except the Blacks. You can defend them all you like," he insisted, "but you're not going to tell me that there's not something wrong with a culture -- or a lack of one -- that consistently gets left behind by everybody else."

Michael abruptly halted his pace.

"So," he said to Peter in a slow, deliberate tone, "you're telling me that the condition of Black people in this country today has nothing to do with slavery?"

"Oh, please," Peter grimaced. "Don't start that again. That was a *long time ago*. It's time to get over it. Get over it!" He raised his hand in a curt farewell and stalked off.

Buffaloes

1918/19

A deadly clatter of machine gun fire shattered the misty silence of the shell-scarred wasteland. Bullets tore through the air above the abandoned trench in which Lieutenant Ralph Brown and the men of the 367th Infantry "Buffalo" Regiment crouched. Soldiers of the 56th Infantry, two hundred yards to Brown's left, shrieked as the German fire found its mark. Another torrent of lead stuttered out of the gun. More screams and anguished cries came from the wounded Americans.

Brown and his men scrambled toward the sound of the gunfire. Brown signaled to a lookout to mount an observation step as another murderous rattle of machine fire rang out. The men of the 56th howled in agony as they were hit again.

Private Fred Babcock peered over the sandbags. "They're tangled in barbed wire," he reported. "Exposed. There's two German guns, three hundred yards to the left, makin mincemeat of em!"

"Gunners," Brown ordered. "Mount your guns. Take out those batteries! Quickly!"

The stricken troops entangled in the barbed wire continued to be riddled by sporadic fire. Brown's men lugged the heavy guns to observation steps and heaved them over the top. First one, then both machine guns came into action, directing withering fire at the enemy positions. The Germans pivoted their aim to return fire. Bullets exploded in the soil all around Brown's gunners. Private Arthur Burton was hit in the neck, his blood and flesh spattering gunner Ernest Robinson's face as the mortally wounded man fell into the trench.

"Christ!" Robinson shrieked. "Ammo, more ammo!" he cried.

Private Alonzo Potter dragged the dying Burton aside and assumed his fallen comrade's position feeding ammunition into the gun.

"Them bastards gonna pay," Robinson snarled, unleashing a furious rain of lead at the enemy.

"Target the one on the right!" hollered the other gunner, Billy Niles.

The two gunners concentrated their fire on one of the German batteries. Cries and strangled screams echoing across the shattered landscape after a few moments told the American gunners that their bullets had found their target.

"The other one!" yelled Robinson, as bullets continued to pepper the earth all around them.

The Americans pivoted their aim, sending a lethal hail of lead into the enemy position. It, too, fell silent, leaving only the crackle of small arms fire and distant rumble of shelling.

Lieutenant Brown scrambled over to the gunners.

"Burton?" he asked.

"Dead," grunted Robinson, wiping his blood-spattered face.

Brown caught sight of Burton's shattered body.

"Jesus!" he winced. "Corpsman!" Brown hollered. "Those men in the barbed wire out there need help! Platoon, we're going over the top to cover the 56th's retirement. Hold the left flank and keep an eye out for snipers. Got it? Here we go," Brown cried, clambering out of the trench at the head of his men.

The engagement at Pagny signaled to Ralph Brown and the men of the 367th Infantry Regiment, 92nd Division, United States Army, that the War was in its final days. The Americans had driven the German Army from the Argonne Forest and were in pursuit as the enemy retreated over open terrain. German lines were collapsing all along the Western front under pressure from an Allied offensive. The armistice came days later. With the fighting over, the 367th was relieved by the French Army, and the troops were ordered to march west to Pont-à-Mousson.

The townspeople of Pont-à-Mousson were giddy with victory and greeted the American soldiers eagerly. Despite heavy destruction, the war-ravaged town assumed a carnival air. Everywhere the men went they were welcomed and celebrated by grateful locals. Lieutenant Egbert Thompson organized a regimental band concert. The hundreds of residents who flocked to the tricolor-draped Place Duroc were moved to tears by the band's renditions of patriotic French tunes. When Thompson struck up a rollicking ragtime set, though, the rousing syncopated rhythm changed the mood entirely, and caused a sensation such as the place had never seen. After four exhausting years of death and destruction, the townspeople were thrilled by the energy and excitement that the black Americans brought to the town.

The two dozen Providence men of the 367th adopted an improvised *auberge* amongst the ruins of the town as their watering hole. They gathered there each off-duty evening, drinking and chatting, and mixing merrily, as much as language permitted, with the locals. The men were delighted to discover that the language barrier proved no hindrance at all to meeting members of the opposite sex.

A group of Providence soldiers bantered with some of the French *poilus* they were billeted with.

"Hey Loic, what'd you say these locals was called again?" Private Otis Champlin asked.

"*Mussipontains*," the French soldier answered.

"Pussimontaines," Otis affected to repeat, to gales of laughter from his comrades.

"No, no!" the *poilu* insisted, which only made Americans laugh harder.

"It's okay, Loic, *d'accord, d'accord*," Otis assured him, laughing.

"I like it my way better."

"Me, too," Cleon Harris gurgled, gulping his beer.

Fred Babcock whistled, catching sight of Leroy Henderson entering the bar with a pretty young woman on his arm.

"Hoo, boy, Leroy, your luck is in," Fred called over.

The lumbering private smiled shyly and retreated to a quiet corner with the girl.

A young Frenchwoman spied Private Alonzo Potter, the regimental band's singer, as he entered the bar. She rushed up and planted a long kiss on his lips.

"*Merci pour la belle musique!*" she gushed as she released him.

"*Merci* yesself," a bemused Alonzo replied.

The young woman turned and called to the assembled Americans.

"*Vive l'Amérique! Vive les Buffaloes! Vive le ragtime!*"

The men all cheered and raised their glasses. Alonzo followed the woman to the bar.

"How'd that girl know we was buffaloes?" asked Cleon Harris.

"Cause we all got buffalo patches on our sleeves, knucklehead," replied Otis Champlin.

"An' guys been telling anybody'd listen how way back the Indians called the colored soldiers that, on account of they fought like charging buffaloes," Billy Niles added.

"Yessir," Ernest Robinson purred, "I'm gonna get me some o' that polly-voo tonight."

"Damn right," Babcock chuckled.

"Them French girls sure like a tall, dark man," Otis Champlin chuckled. "Hot dog! I tell you, they been all over me."

"Yeah, like flies to a pile of road apples some old mare left behind," Robinson wisecracked.

Otis swatted Ernest with his cap.

"You want another beer?" he asked.

"If you're payin, I'm stayin," Ernest replied.

Hours passed. Men bought drinks for local women, and they drifted away in pairs. A little after ten, after walking his sweetheart home, Leroy Henderson rejoined the small group of his comrades remaining.

"Your girl's nice, Leroy," Alonzo Potter said, as Leroy slumped into a seat, looking miserable.

"Sure is," Dick Tapscott added. "A real cutie."

"Yeah," Leroy replied glumly. "Hey, you guys think we gonna be shipping out soon, like everybody's sayin?"

"Bound to," Alonzo replied. "This is too good to last, that's for sure."

"If a good thing can be screwed up," agreed Dick, "the U.S. Army'll find a way to."

"But I don't wanna go back," Leroy said. "I want to marry Claudine."

"Jeez, Leon, how you gonna do that?" Alonzo responded. "It's not as if you can stay,"

Leroy gazed into the distance morosely.

"I'll run away," he said.

Alonzo snorted.

"Desert? That'd be plain dumb," he said. "A colored man in France? You'd be caught in no time. You'll lose that girl of yours and get yourself nothin but a long stretch in Leavenworth."

"Yeah, man, keep your cool. Just enjoy yourself," Dick said. "The other guys is all doin it."

"But I *love* her," Leon insisted.

"Yeah, well, the army ain't givin you no choice," Dick retorted.

Tears welled in Leroy's eyes.

"I like it better over here," he moaned. "People are different. They're just *normal* with you, not like back home."

"They sure are friendly," Alonzo agreed.

"Them French girls is crazy for your singin," Dick said.

"That's not the only thing they're crazy for," Alonzo laughed. "Leroy's right, though, these French people? They're different. They just love our music. Doesn't matter to em that it's a colored band playing it. In fact, I think they're actually more interested in the music *because* a colored band's playin it. We got *energy*, and they like it. People are *interested,* they want to get to know us."

"That's what I'm saying," Leroy said. "It's like… a *different world* from back home. I just wish I could stay."

"What'd I just say about the army screwing a good thing up? T'ain't no one askin you," Dick said.

"Would *you* stay, if you could?" Leroy asked Alonzo.

Alonzo thought for a moment.

"Nah," he replied, shaking his head. "I couldn't stand to be so far away from my family. But I'm real glad I got to come here and meet the people and do all the things we did."

"Yeah," agreed Leroy.

"Me, too," Dick sighed.

Alonzo seemed lost in thought.

"I see things now with different eyes," he murmured.

In a smoke-filled barracks on the outskirts of town, an assembly of American officers was receiving orders. Colonel Gardiner of the 56th Infantry, in command of the troop train that would be transporting the 56th and 367th Infantry Regiments, read the wired orders directing units to travel to the embarkation point at Brest the following day.

"We marshal at the station at zero-eight hundred hours," he announced. "The special train departs at nine-thirty."

"Accommodation assignments are being distributed," Gardiner continued, as his aide-de-camp handed out copies. "First class carriages for officers, second class for white enlisted men, boxcars for the negroes."

"Boxcars?" Lieutenant Ralph Brown blurted out.

The colonel angrily scanned the room.

"Who said that?" he asked.

Brown rose and saluted.

"Me, sir," he answered. "Begging you pardon, sir, but why boxcars for the colored men?"

"Because those are my orders," the colonel growled.

"But, sir, our men have fought as bravely as any others."

The colonel's face flushed.

"Who's this man's superior officer?" he barked.

Major Armstrong of the 367th stood up.

"Me, sir," he replied.

"I don't take kindly to insubordination, major, especially not from no negro. I'll see the two of you directly after this briefing."

Lieutenant Egbert Thompson leaned over to Brown as he resumed his seat.

"You're in for it now," he hissed. "Are you crazy?"

"I thought we'd put this damned foolishness to bed," Brown whispered.

"Yeah, well, think again," Thompson muttered.

Major Armstrong had a face like thunder as the meeting broke up. Like all of the 367th's officers above the rank of captain, Armstrong was white.

"You just can't keep that mouth of yours shut, can you, Brown?" Armstrong said. "Well, you've picked the wrong man to get into a pissing contest with this time. Gardiner's a good old boy from Tennessee. He'd sooner string you up than give you a fair hearing. What were you thinking?"

"I was thinking, sir, that if we don't stand up for ourselves, who will?"

"You're out of line, Brown. You know I've always gone the extra mile for your men."

"Like on the troopship, when they got fed twice a day while the white men got three meals?" Brown asked.

"And your boys kicked up a fuss, and got the firehoses turned on them? A lot of good that did them. Spent the whole night soaked to the skin and shivering."

Armstrong softened his tone.

"Look, Ralph, you and the men fought bravely. Your unit received a commendation for it. Don't make it worse for the men, or yourself. Please—just let me do the talking with Gardiner."

The two men approached the colonel.

"Major Armstrong and Lieutenant Brown of the 367th, sir, reporting as ordered," Armstrong said, saluting.

Colonel Gardiner scowled at Brown.

"Can't you keep this hothead under control, major?" he demanded.

"Sir, in my opinion, Lieutenant Brown is justifiably aggrieved that his men are to travel to Brest in boxcars."

"Gotta put 'em somewhere," Gardiner grunted. "Besides, we don't want fights breaking out. There's always trouble when whites and coloreds mix."

"Why would there be trouble, sir?" Brown asked.

Major Armstrong silently rolled his eyes.

"Our men are billeted with French soldiers right now," Brown continued, "and there's no trouble. In fact, they're getting on famously."

The colonel bristled.

"My boys are from the *South*," he replied. "From Texas, Mississippi, Tennessee. We don't stand mixing with coloreds."

"Your boys didn't mind mixing with us at Pagny, sir," Brown retorted. "When we saved them from those German gunners."

"Damn fools," Gardiner muttered. "You probably blundered into them Germans."

Brown grasp on the cap in his hands tightened.

"I've heard tell," the colonel recounted, "that when negro soldiers first met the Germans, they threw down their rifles and set on them with street razors."

"That's a lie, sir, a malicious lie," Brown said.

The colonel raised his eyebrows, glancing at Armstrong.

"Your coon talks like a Philadelphia lawyer, major," he chuckled.

"A Providence lawyer, in fact," Brown responded. "Providence, Rhode Island."

Gardiner chuckled again.

"Well, I'll be," he said. "A coon lawyer from Providence, Rhode Island."

The colonel looked Brown up and down.

"They sure are *natty* dressers, aren't they, major? Take real *pride* in their appearance. Why, I haven't seen such shiny boots outside of G.H.Q. Colored officers!" Gardiner snorted. "Good for nuthin but struttin around and showing off. What'd you put this one in charge of? Digging latrines?"

"Lieutenant Brown and his men got a commendation for the action at Pagny, sir," Armstrong replied.

"Is that so? Well, I suppose I ought t'thank you, *Lieutenant* Brown," Gardiner said with exaggerated courtesy. "Though it still don't sit right with me. You know, major, between you and me, I think top brass made a big mistake appointin colored officers. Made em big headed. They've been *spoiled* over here, like the rest of the coloreds, spoiled by mixin with people who don't know what they're like, and mixin with women they got no business mixin with."

Colonel Gardiner lit a cigar.

"Everyone knows the colored soldier is an ignoramus," he said, puffing. "And likely as not a rapist."

Brown trembled with rage.

The colonel chortled, exulting in Brown's humiliation.

"That's right, son," he said. "Colored soldiers ain't been worth a *damn* over here. Oh, the big bucks, them huskies, they can unload cargo or dig trenches-- a lot of em worked on levees in the South. But they ain't worth *shit* as fighting men. There ain't been a colored soldier worth his salt's fought on French soil."

"Does that include the ones *under* it?" Brown asked.

The colonel's face went crimson, his temples bulging.

"Major," he snarled, "get this uppity piece of shit out of here. He can tell his colored fellas that they're going to stay locked in a boxcar until we reach Brest, where they're gonna board a segregated transport to ship em back to the segregated U-nited States. Is that clear?"

"Yes, sir," Armstrong answered.

"Goddamn negroes got to learn their place again," the colonel fumed. "Dismissed."

Armstrong and Brown walked back to their quarters in the

darkness.

"He's right about one thing, you know," Armstrong said. "You fellas can't carry on the way you've been doing here. People back home won't stand it."

"We need to learn our place again, like the colonel said, is that it?" asked Brown.

"You will if you know what's good for you," the major replied wearily. "Good night, Brown."

Hordes of troops and well-wishers crowded the platform at Pont-à-Mousson station the next morning, where a locomotive chuffed, waiting to transport the American troops to Brest. Women ladled out soup from vast, steaming cauldrons, and children ran along the train to sit on the American soldiers' laps one last time and bid them bon voyage. Lovers exchanged tearful farewells. The 367th regimental band played a farewell set of spirited ragtime numbers.

Marshals began slowly guiding troops along the train. The men of the 367th were directed to a boxcar at its end. Ralph Brown shuffled along with his men. A non-commissioned officer by the boxcar stopped him as he was about to enter.

"Colored officers' accommodation is towards the front, sir," the serjeant said.

"I'm where I belong, soldier," Brown told the sentry.

The freezing boxcar stank of hay and manure. Men hung lanterns and broke up discarded crates to light a fire in a small stove in a corner of the car. Soldiers sprawled on the floor in their overcoats, propping themselves on their duffel bags. After an hour's wait, the locomotive whistled and the train lurched into motion.

The men gabbled noisily as the train clattered along the track, gathering speed.

"How come you ain't ridin with the off'cers, sir?" Alonzo Potter asked Brown.

"I'll tell you, Potter, I'll tell all of you."

Brown stood and gave a long, loud whistle to quieten the din of conversation.

"Fellas," he shouted, "I'm here to tell you… I'm here to tell you that I went to bat for you, and I struck out. See, there's a son of a bitch Tennessee colonel in charge of this train who's determined to see to it that we're put in our place. Well, I'm in my place."

The men stamped their feet appreciatively, hooting and whistling.

"We're headed back home," Brown said, "But we're headed back as different men than the ones who set out. Combat has changed us. You men have proved that we can't be outmatched by any white soldier."

"That's right," voices agreed.

"We sure as Hell earned the Germans' respect," Brown said, to an exultant roar from the men.

"And we won the friendship of the French," he continued. "And our time in France has changed us, too. We've tasted equality here, manhood on an equal basis, *common decency*-- and we'll never go back to accepting less."

The boxcar thundered with shouts and stamping feet.

"We've earned the respect of everybody, all except our American brothers-in-arms. Men, bigots like that colonel tell us that we're not worthy of the rights—our constitutional rights-- that they try to deny us. Well, what you men have done over here has swept that notion away. Demolished it."

The men roared in affirmation.

"They can put us in a boxcar, but we'll never go back to their Jim Crow box. We've proved our worth as equal citizens beyond any doubt. And that's why I'm here, riding with you: to tell you the truth. I'm here to tell you that *there's nothing wrong with us*! What's wrong is with the country that we're headed back to! Forget about making the *world* safe for democracy like President Wilson says, it's time that we cleaned our own house. Why not make *America* safe for democracy?"

The hurricane of cheers continued.

"We return from fighting, brothers," Brown thundered, raising his fist. "We *return fighting*."

In memory of African American Rhode Islanders who served in World War I, among whom were:

Elmer Leon Blockson, of Providence, who served a term as commander of the (segregated) Burton-Perry Post of the Veterans of Foreign Wars (VFW), named in honor of World War I casualties Arthur Burton and Eugene Perry. He sat on national committees of the VFW and was Chief Marshal of Providence's Armistice Day parade in 1962.

Benjamin Branner, of Providence, a railroad worker, who was active in the (segregated) Order of Elks. In 1942, he spearheaded a petition calling on the city to appoint Black police officers. He died in 1979.

Arthur Burton, of Providence, who died of wounds sustained in the Meuse-Argonne offensive in 1918.

Robert T. Hickman, of Providence, an elevator operator, who was a founder and six-term commander of the Burton-Perry VFW Post. At the time of his death in 1969, his son, Robert, Jr., was serving in the Vietnam War.

John R. Jones, of Providence, a street sweeper operator who was a founder and one-time commander of the Burton-Perry VFW Post. He died in 1952.

Richard S. Lindsey, of Providence, a chauffeur and cab driver, Mason, and one-time commander of the Burton-Perry VFW Post. He was the father of ten, grandfather of fifty-three, and great-grandfather of 122. He died in 1980.

Asa Mars, a custodian at the *Providence Journal,* who was a prominent church soloist and singer with the Excelsior Quartet, which performed at civic events. His wife, Ella, was treasurer of the Providence branch of the NAACP. He died in 1965.

Eugene Perry, of Cranston, who died of influenza in France in 1918.

Elmer P. Sawyer, of Providence, who received a commission in 1918 and served as a lieutenant with the 367th Infantry. A career officer, he was ultimately appointed colonel in command of the 15th Regiment, New York National Guard. When he died in 1942, his flag-draped casket returned to Providence for burial, accompanied by three carloads of flowers. His son, and namesake, served in World War II.

James M. Stockett, Jr, of Providence, who was admitted to the Rhode Island bar in 1911. He received a commission in 1918 and served as a lieutenant with the 367th Infantry. On returning to civilian life, Stockett became a prominent lawyer and advocate for Rhode Island's African American community, playing a role in the foundation of the Crispus Attucks Association, a civic welfare organization now known as the John Hope Settlement House. He died in 1945.

Robert H. Walker, of Providence, who served a term as commander of the Burton-Perry VFW Post. He was an air raid warden in World War II and an active member of the Congdon Street Baptist Church congregation.

Afterword

I have a friend (quite a good friend) who tells me— "We don't need people like *you* to tell our stories. We can tell our own stories." I understand exactly where he's coming from. Black people have been denied their own voices for far too long and have had quite enough of being *spoken for* by White people like me. African Americans are justifiably fed up with White creators expropriating their vibrant culture for profit (as Whites have done for centuries). Yet... I feel bound to respond to the objection, as I do to my friend, with a question: "If I was an archaeologist, and I unearthed an artifact of importance to African American history, what should I do? Put it back in the ground where I found it and cover it up with soil, for a Black archaeologist to possibly discover at some point in the future?"

Perhaps I was naïve, but when I began this project, I did not appreciate the depth of the taboo surrounding White authors writing Black characters. This virtual prohibition was, I believe, the principal reason that no one in the publishing industry would countenance touching this work, alongside the fact that, as one literary agent confided to me, though publishers affect to clamor for stories about underrepresented voices, the truth is that the publishing industry caters almost exclusively to the tastes of a White audience.

The realization of my blunder came a bit late in the day for me. I had done the research; I had written the stories. What was I to do? Was it better to press ahead and recount the real-life experiences of Okyerema Mireku, Thomas Howland, and the African captives aboard the *Little George*, or to leave their stories untold?

Slavery's long shadow touches the lives of White Americans no less than it does those of Blacks, because the transatlantic slave trade necessitated the invention of the concept of Whiteness. This "racial" construct, in turn, gave birth to its corollary, White supremacy, which informs a socialization narrative of inequality, inferiority, and inhumanity that is internalized to one extent or another by each one of us. This intellectual and cultural legacy of slavery, and fear of the erosion of its predominance in the twenty-first century, it seems to me, lies at the heart of a growing sense of White victimhood, the appeal of Donald Trump and his imitators abroad, and indeed, of the need to assert that "Black Lives Matter" at all.

It has been nearly forty years since the scholar Peggy McIntosh unpacked that invisible knapsack of White privilege, containing the passports, codebooks, secret passwords, and blank checks with which White people are equipped to navigate the world. Among those Whites conscious of the phenomenon at all, White privilege remains a contested concept for some and is blithely accepted as "the norm" by many more. A preponderance of Whites, probably, consider themselves to be the fortunate recipients of an accident of birth, shrug their shoulders, and get on with their lives.

For those who still need the contents of that knapsack sifting through, I am talking about privileges like being born to parents who had access to jobs, and the consequent advantages growing up in a privileged position, in terms of housing, security, and education. I am talking about the better jobs, higher salaries, and more generous pensions that this start in life set them up for, generational wealth inherited by some, financial security, better healthcare, longer lives, and opportunities to amass wealth to pass on to their descendants. And these are only the economic dimensions. White privilege is an array of societal structures, institutions, cultural norms, and belief systems that set Whites up to flourish, in relative terms, while disadvantaging other groups, especially African Americans. The concepts of Whiteness and White privilege, in their manifold forms, are a direct legacy of slavery and the transatlantic trade in enslaved African people, and, in my view, *are the source of many of the worst evils of the modern world.*

Acknowledgment of this fact has nothing to do with feeling guilty about being White. It is, rather, about taking responsibility for our history and not being complacent about the impact of its presence in our lives today. As McIntosh wrote all those years ago, until we White people decide what each of us must do to lessen our unearned privilege, or to end it, we are part of the problem. I say that we Whites cross the line from being personally blameless for a ghastly history to becoming complicit in it when we do not disavow our inheritance of slavery, White privilege. To do anything less than playing our part in dismantling structures that disadvantage people of African heritage is to openly confess our racism. As the distinguished academic Ibram X. Kendi argues, one can either be racist or anti-racist, there are no other choices.

I touch upon the contentious subject of reparations for slavery only to cite a historical precedent that may be unfamiliar to some American readers. When slavery was abolished in the British Empire in 1833, there was widespread recognition that a grave injustice had been done, and a political consensus emerged that recompense must be made. Thus, the British government, in an unprecedented step, paid the gargantuan sum of £20,000,000 (at least seventeen billion dollars in today's money) in compensation to the slaves' *former owners* for being deprived of their property. I raise this by way of analogy, to point out that where there is political will, objections of expense or impracticality are not insurmountable.

The fact that you are reading this provides my answer to the conundrum of the White archaeologist and the artifact: I have decided to publish and be damned. Others can judge the propriety of my choice. I will gladly accept criticism, or even censure, if that is the price of getting us talking about the darker side of our shared history, and about what we, as individuals, must do about the living legacy of slavery that affects the lives of each one of us.

Acknowledgments

I am deeply grateful to Robert Taylor, Dinzey Walters, Vernal Scott, Erin Littlewood, Jim Metcalfe, and Christine Trottier for their thoughtful comments on this text. Frank critiques from people dear to me shaped this work for the better and reinforced my already-strong sense that these stories needed to be told.

I thank Joseph Wright for challenging the propriety of my authorship with his characteristic candor. Joe's obstinate objections prompted me to grapple with an elephant in the room (see Afterword) and re-examine the text with heightened sensitivity. I am indebted to Ibrahim Njai for his on-the-ground insights into Sierra Leonean culture and geography, and for the friendship that has blossomed as a result. Though Professors Matthew Kelly and Paul Readman have no knowledge of this work, I owe them both an enormous debt of gratitude for starting me out on what has proved an endlessly rewarding path.

I acknowledge with thanks permission to reproduce Ernest Hamlin Baker's *Economic Activities in the Days of the Narragansett Planters* granted by the United States Postal Service. John Blanchard's portrait of Thomas Howland, with which Baker's mural shares the cover, appears courtesy of the Rhode Island Historical Society.

My mother, Constance Connery, is, as always, an inexhaustible source of support and encouragement for all that I do. A natural teacher, she is, at an advanced age, still helping others in ways that she can. To have a mother like mine has been a blessing beyond words.

I am grateful to Ravindran Vadivelu (with a wink to Wodehouse), without whose expansive discourse and illuminative asides this book would have been finished in half the time.

The tasks involved in writing this, were aided, in one way or another, by the support of cherished friends and family: Erin and Tom Littlewood, Jen and Matt Krenz-Erni, James Erni and Kristin Taylor, Mary Anne Breed, David Adams, Darlene Adams, Azad Khaleel and Goran Savic, Edilson Guerreiro and Arnt Stubberud, Jim Metcalfe (and Peg), Wijay Pitumpe and Philip Lightowlers, Scott and Alexandra Davidson, Billy Ray, Richard Trottier, Geetha and Stuart Parker, Keira Naran and Wesley Gusterson, Mireya Leudo Arenas, Manickavel Vadiveloo, Dominic Beazer, Bilaal Tariq, Javier Asperilla de la Llave, Atle Borøchstein, Jelani Pantor, Peter Bennett, Canniggia Goodluck, Richard Cooke, and Jonathan Williams.

This book is dedicated to my dear friend of four decades, Gary Adams. My deep affection for Gary, and contemplation of the descent into darkness that we are witnessing, more or less compelled me to write these stories.

About the Author

Native Rhode Islander James Doherty is a graduate of Washington University in St Louis and King's College London. He holds a Ph.D. in history from the University of Southampton. A frequent visitor to his beloved home state, James lives in London.

Further Reading

Christy Clark-Pujara, *Dark Work: the business of slavery in Rhode Island*

Jay Coughtry, *The Notorious Triangle*

John Crouch, "Providence Newspapers and the Racist Riots of 1824 and 1831"

Paul Davis, "The Unrighteous Traffic, Rhode Island and the Slave Trade", five-part series in the *Providence Journal*, March 12-19, 2006

Eli Ginzburg and Alfred S. Eichner, *Troublesome Presence: Democracy and Black Americans*

Joanne Pope Melish, *Disowning Slavery: Gradual Emancipation and "Race" in New England, 1780–1860*

William H. Robinson, ed., *The Proceedings of the Free African Union Society and the African Benevolent Society, Newport, Rhode Island 1780-1824*

Rowena Stewart, *A Heritage Discovered: Blacks in Rhode Island*

Keith Stokes, *A Matter of Truth: the struggle for African heritage & indigenous people equal rights in Providence, Rhode Island (1620-2020)*

Richard C. Youngken, *African Americans in Newport*

And lots more on smallstatebighistory.com

USPS Disclaimer Statement for Murals

The Postal Service respects and embraces the uniqueness and diversity of every individual. And we encourage contributions of people from different backgrounds, experiences, and perspectives, including those of our employees and members of the communities we serve.

Between 1934 and 1943, the U.S. Treasury Department, as part of President Franklin Roosevelt's New Deal program, commissioned more than 1,400 pieces of artwork to be created and installed in Post Office locations around the country for permanent public display. Traditionally, Post Office lobbies were frequently visited by community members from all walks of life, making those locations particularly accessible display sites for artwork.

While it is the policy of the Postal Service to preserve and protect the historic artwork in its collection for future generations, we are mindful that certain murals generate strong feelings for some of our employees and customers.

With that in mind, the Postal Service is working with the Smithsonian Institution to properly handle and safeguard the future of those pieces. We are evaluating identified pieces, and we will work to ensure that appropriate action is taken on the select murals, including the possible installation of interpretive text near some of the murals, if deemed necessary.

United States Postal Service® 2025